HOLY TERROR IN THE HEBRIDES

A Dorothy Martin Mystery

*Also by Jeanne M. Dams
in Large Print:*

The Body in the Transept
Trouble in the Town Hall

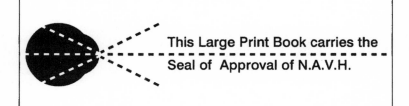

HOLY TERROR IN THE HEBRIDES

A Dorothy Martin Mystery

JEANNE M. DAMS

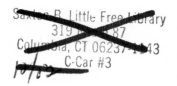
Thorndike Press • Thorndike, Maine

This book is a work of fiction. The characters, incidents, and dialogues are products of the author's imagination and are not to be construed as real. Any resemblance to actual events or persons, living or dead, is entirely coincidental.

Published in 2000 in Large Print by arrangement with Walker Publishing Company, Inc.

Thorndike Press Large Print Senior Lifestyles Series.

The tree indicium is a trademark of Thorndike Press.

The text of this Large Print edition is unabridged.
Other aspects of the book may vary from the original edition.

Set in 16 pt. Plantin by Susan Guthrie.

Printed in the United States on permanent paper.

Library of Congress Cataloging-in-Publication Data

Dams, Jeanne M.
    Holy terror in the Hebrides : a Dorothy Martin Mystery / Jeanne M. Dams.
        p. (large print) cm.
    ISBN 0-7862-2407-X (lg. print : hc : alk. paper)
    1. Martin, Dorothy (Fictitious character) — Fiction.
2. Women detectives — Scotland — Fiction. 3. Iona (Scotland) — Fiction. 4. Large type books. I. Title.
PS3554.A498 H65 2000
813'.54—dc21   99-089095

Acknowledgments

As Dorothy L. Sayers said with reference to Oxford, it would be idle to deny that the Isle of Iona does actually exist, and very largely as I have portrayed it. I've run up a house or two and had the temerity to turn a large house owned by the Abbey into a hotel, but those fortunate enough to know Iona will certainly recognize it.

And, as the island shelters no more than ninety some full-time residents, it would be equally useless to pretend that none of them served as inspiration for my characters. In particular, masquerading under the name of MacPherson goes David Kirkpatrick, whose family has operated the Staffa boat for generations, time out of mind. (I have never met his wife, but I have no doubt she brews excellent tea.) I hasten to add that all foolish or unpleasant characters, English, Scottish, or American, are the products solely of my imagination.

To the people of Iona, then, and to all those hardy Christian souls from St. Columba onward whose benevolent influences have endowed Iona with a peace so vast that only the tortuous mind of a mystery writer could conceive of murderous intent along its shores, this book is gratefully dedicated. I must, however, also mention my deep debt of gratitude to Michael Seidman, without whose inspired editing this hymn to Iona would have been much the poorer.

1

If the universe behaved in the foreshadowing manner it used to in thirties thrillers, a thunderstorm would have been in progress, or threatening, or at the very least clouds would have been gathering as the little bus jolted over the road across Mull. But weather these days seems to have abandoned its role as a prophet of doom. After, admittedly, a rather gray dawn, Scotland had pulled itself together and put on its best face for its tourists. The brisk sunshine positively sparkled, with that crystalline quality of the very best autumn days. I bounced along, holding on to my hat and trying not to let my head hit the roof, uncomfortable but deeply content. Sighing with pure pleasure, I gazed out the window, wishing the bus would stop long enough for me to trap the view in my memory forever.

On either side of the road, rugged slopes of rocky meadowland soared sharply to the sky, with now and then a narrow stream — "burns" they were called in Scotland, I remembered — tumbling down in a mad rush of white water. Sheep grazed here and there, keeping their footing by magic, apparently, and wandering across the road when they felt like it. I found their meanderings charming; the bus driver didn't, but he managed not to hit any, also presumably by magic. Pheasants and grouse (or so this ignorant, town-bred American supposed) whirred up every so often in colorful display, and once a small herd of stags leapt across the road, achingly beautiful with their magnificent racks of antlers and their proud bearing, like dancers, like kings.

I was crossing the island of Mull in the Scottish Hebrides, and doing it on a bus, because of a complicated series of events. I've never quite understood why my life tends to complications. Other people seem able to get organized, but even after sixty-odd years of trying to live tidily, I find myself in one entanglement after another. To begin with, my four-hundred-year-old house in the southeast of England was being renovated, and the mess had just reached the unbearable stage when the Andersons (friends and fellow American expatriates; they live in London) called to invite me to spend a couple of weeks with them on the tiny island of Iona.

"It's a *magical* place, Dorothy," said Lynn

in her emphatic Katharine Hepburn style; I could picture her thin, elegant hands waving at the other end of the line. "Rocky hills with lots of sheep, air like wine, fuchsia hedges growing twelve feet tall, I *swear* . . ."

"Come on! Fuchsias? In Scotland?"

"It's the Gulf Stream, D.," Tom chimed in on the extension. "Keeps the weather much more temperate than you'd expect that far north. And for once my charming wife isn't exaggerating. The hedges do grow at least that high, and they're covered with blooms this time of year. And you know I haven't got any imagination, but there's something about the atmosphere of the place . . . anyway, you'd love it. We've rented a cottage, and there's room for three."

"There's lots of fresh crab, Dorothy, and the most *exquisite* salmon!"

That did it. Lynn knows my weaknesses, and unfortunately the palate is one of them. Despite my constant efforts to be sensible, my figure shows my deep and abiding love for good food. And then there was the dust and noise of rebuilding — and besides, I was lonesome. My dear friend, or . . . well, dear friend would do . . . Chief Constable Alan Nesbitt, was away in Brussels at a European Community police conference, and I was at loose ends.

"We-ell . . ." I said to the telephone.

"Good! Be sure to pack warm clothes, sensible stuff — sweaters and slacks. It can get cold even in the summer on Iona, let alone in September, and nobody ever dresses up. We're leaving a week from Monday; we'll call and let you know when we'll pick you up. And Dorothy, we're *so* glad you're coming!"

I'd limited my shopping to the recommended sensible clothes, indulging in my passion for hats with just one jaunty tam-o'-shanter affair in red velvet with a tartan band and a feather cockade, and happily told my boss at my volunteer job that I'd be away for a while. But the phone call, when it came a few days later, was to tell me that Tom was suffering severe chest pains and had been sent to the hospital. "His doctor wants to watch him, Dorothy," said Lynn, as subdued as I'd ever heard her. "He says it's probably not an actual heart attack, but he's been warning Tom for years that he needs to lose weight and get more exercise, and this is a good excuse to run a lot of tests and see just what the situation is. I — I'm sort of scared." She sounded more like a little girl than the wealthy, witty, self-assured society woman I'd known for years.

"I can sympathize," I said with feeling.

My husband, Frank, had died of a heart attack that had come with no such warning. But Lynn didn't need right now to be reminded of my experience. "Do try not to fret yourself into a state, Lynn. That won't help Tom at all. Look upon this as a fire alarm, a chance for Tom to get out safely."

"Well, at least I can finally make him go on a diet," she said with a hint of familiar determination. "But we both feel so badly about letting you down."

"Good grief, Lynn!"

"Yes, I know, but we do. Look, why don't you go ahead anyway? I know you won't want to drive, but the train connections aren't too bad. We looked them up. And the cottage is already paid for; it'd be a shame to waste it. We might be able to join you later, when Tom is feeling better. I know he'll just go on stewing about it if you don't go."

Lynn was right about the driving. Driving in the UK, even after living here for over a year, is for me an exquisitely refined torture. But I *had* begun to look forward to getting away, and Tom *wouldn't* cure himself by worrying. So I packed my sweaters and slacks (and long underwear just in case), made arrangements with my amiable next-door neighbor Jane Langland to look after my two cats, and hopped on the train to

11

London for the first leg of a trip that would involve two more trains, a ferry, a bus, and another ferry, with an overnight stay in the little port town of Oban. The entire distance to be covered was less than five hundred miles as the crow flies, but distances are relative. In Britain they can take a lot longer to cover than in America.

Now, though, I was nearing my journey's end. I glanced at my watch. In fifteen minutes or so we'd arrive at the tiny village of Fionnphort (pronounced, oddly, *finna-fort*) to catch the ferry to Iona. The landscape was beginning to flatten out and grow less interesting as we made the descent toward the sea, and I'd been up at six, to catch the seven o'clock ferry from Oban. I stretched out my legs and closed my eyes.

I suppose the conversation behind me had been going on for some time, but I hadn't noticed. Now, with my eyes shut, I couldn't seem to ignore it.

"Can't say I care much what they do with each other, but with AIDS and all that these days, I'd just as soon not have to mix with them." It was a rather flat voice, American in accent, low in volume, but irritated enough to carry.

"An abomination unto the Lord!" The second voice, also American, was rich and deep, a warm contralto. " 'Men with men workin' that which is unseemly.' Romans 1:27. But never you mind, Sister Douglas, the Lord'll strike 'em down in His own good time. He says —"

The bus driver changed gears to negotiate a sharp bend onto a narrow stone bridge, and the rest was mercifully drowned out in the roar of the engine and the beat of tires over cobblestones. I sat up again and looked out the window unhappily. The nastiness of the little exchange I'd overheard had blighted the view. I wondered what they looked like, these rather unpleasant compatriots of mine, but I didn't glance back. If I caught their eye, they might draw me into a discussion I wanted no part of.

And then we were hurtling down a steep street that ended near the water's edge in a parking lot full of cars and tour buses. Our driver pulled up next to a green-and-cream behemoth and applied his hand brake with a screech.

"End of the road, ladies and gentlemen," he announced in a strong Scottish accent. "If ye're goin' to Iona juist for the day, the last bus for Craignure leaves at two forty-five; ye'll want to catch the two-thirty ferry. And I want ye to know, yon deer were laid on specially for your entertainment. No extra charge!"

Amid the laughter I heard several American voices asking, "What did he say?" A good many of my countrymen were apparently traveling to Iona today. Maybe, I thought hopefully, the disagreeable pair were on a day trip, and I wouldn't run into them again. As we all got off the bus I gave them a casual glance. They looked all right, a wiry little woman with a tanned, weatherbeaten face, dressed in a rumpled khaki jacket and pants, and a large, amiable-looking black woman, her comfortable folds encased in a bright pink sweat suit. All the same . . .

I straightened my hat, collected my luggage, and walked the few steps to the boat that was waiting for us at the jetty.

It was the tiniest excuse for a ferry I'd ever seen. There was room for two cars, maybe three if they were all subcompacts. No wonder tourists couldn't take cars over! Only one vehicle was making the crossing this time, and after it was situated, the foot passengers boarded by the same ramp, getting our feet a little wet as a wave curled up under the boat and licked the jetty. Most of the car deck was open to the sky, but there was a steep ladder leading to the rudimentary upper deck that circled the boat, so I abandoned my bags and climbed.

This was a true British Tourist Authority kind of day. The sun glinted off the waves, the ultra-blue sky held only a few decorative clouds, artfully positioned, and the chill, salty air was a tonic. I could feel my town-tainted lungs growing cleaner with every breath. Gulls screamed overhead, a stirring sound for those of us who must spend most of our lives far inland. I sighed happily and surveyed the horizon.

There, dead ahead as the boat left its harbor and veered out into Iona Sound, was the fabled Isle of Iona, spread out before me, drawing nearer every moment.

I'd done some reading about Iona. Its important history goes back to the year 563, when a monk named Columba established a monastery there from which Christianity spread to all Scotland. The island is tiny, about four miles long by a mile or so wide, and from where I stood in the bow of the ferry it looked even smaller than I'd imagined; I could see both ends of it. The Abbey was unmistakable, the only substantial building in sight. In fact, aside from a little clutter running along the middle of the near shore, presumably houses and shops, there were no other buildings visible at all. I could unfocus my eyes a little and imagine the island as it must have looked when St.

Columba, not yet a saint, just a monkish exile from Ireland, approached it with his fellow monks in their frail little boat. Except, of course, coming from the south, it would be another viewpoint he got —

"Just like the Irish to send a saint off to a bleak place like this, isn't it?"

The accents were American, and belligerent. I turned, a little startled. A young woman in blue jeans and T-shirt had come up behind me and was surveying Iona with a critical look. In her twenties, I guessed, tall, slender, and very attractive, or she could have been if she'd made any sort of effort. All the effort seemed to be in the other direction, however. Her curly, dark hair was cut short, no makeup sullied her pale cheeks or lovely, dark eyes, and her clothes were much too large for her. She disdained any kind of sweater or jacket, despite the brisk wind. Her backpack was businesslike and wellworn.

"I'm afraid I don't know a lot about the Irish, actually. Are you — ?"

"Italian-American. Teresa Colapietro." She held out a hard, cold hand and gripped mine firmly.

"Dorothy Martin. You seem to know something of Iona's history. I'm afraid I'd never heard of it until a week or so ago, so

16

I've only read a little."

"If you can believe what you read. Most religious history is a load of crap. Miracles, cures, who-knows-what, all performed by a lot of dead white males, and written down by a lot more of them."

A pugnacious attitude always makes me take the opposite point of view. "But surely there are many famous women in the history of the Church. I mean, take Teresa of Avila, for example —"

Her namesake shrugged off Teresa of Avila. "Hysterical. If reported correctly, which isn't likely. The original pack of male chauvinists, that's the Church. Now when God gets Her way, and women get to be priests and cardinals and popes, it'll be a different story. I'm a nun, by the way, Congregation of St. Hortense, but don't bother to call me 'sister'; I don't believe in titles for the religious."

Well! I'd known that some of the new nuns were pretty political, but I was taken aback, all the same. Fortunately, I didn't have to come up with a reply. A series of loud clunks from below meant the big car hatch was opening; we were there.

"See you later." Teresa-not-of-Avila waved and sprinted down the ladder. I followed at a creakier pace. By the time I'd remembered where I'd put my luggage and found my ticket to show as I disembarked, I was the last one off the boat.

I don't know exactly what I'd expected, but the scene on the jetty wasn't it. Of course there weren't any taxis lined up to meet the boat; this wasn't a city. My reading had told me that there were only about ninety inhabitants of the island, most of them crofters — part-time farmers. But how was I to get my luggage to the cottage?

The only transportation I could see was a couple of horsedrawn wagons lined up behind a sign advertising tours of the island. They looked appealing; the horses were well-groomed animals, the wagons clean and freshly painted. I approached the first one, driven by an attractive young woman.

"I'm staying in a cottage some friends rented for a couple of weeks. They said it's at the end of the road, and I'm not sure I can carry my bags that far. Dove Cottage, it is. Could you take me there?"

"Surely," she said, her voice soft and lilting. "Climb up; I'll see to the bags." She dealt easily with the suitcases, climbed onto the driver's perch, and clucked to her horse, who woke from his gentle snooze, obediently wheeled the wagon around, and headed up the village street.

"Why 'Dove Cottage,' by the way? Does it have a dovecote or something?"

My driver chuckled. "Ye'll find a good many things on Iona have to do with doves. 'Iona' means 'dove,' ye see, in Hebrew. And 'Columba' is 'dove' in Latin."

"What a coincidence, then, that Columba happened to come here. Or does the name of the island date from after he came?"

She shrugged. "That's the sort of thing ye might ask the people at the Heritage Centre. They know the history of this island back millions o' years to when it thrust oot o' the sea. I'll show ye the centre, if ye like."

"I'd like that very much, but later, perhaps. I'm tired, and I want to get settled."

We rode past small houses on our left, while on our right gardens stretched down to the sea in a riot of color. There were all kinds: well-disciplined gardens with roses and neatly clipped lawns, gardens left to their own sweet will with wildflowers, heather, and several different kinds of thistle, one untended garden that was little more than a weed patch, but all of them bright with blossoms. And, sure enough, hedges of fuchsia towered everywhere, so thick with purple-and-magenta blossoms that I could hardly see the leaves, and so sweetly scented that a sort of living veil of bees surrounded them. I decided to admire them from a discreet distance.

Just before the narrow street became someone's drive, my driver pulled her horse to a stop. "Here we are, then. Dove Cottage. If ye have your key, I'll help ye with the bags."

I stayed where I was, on the high backseat of the wagon, in a sudden horrified paralysis.

My key. The key Lynn had driven down from London especially to give me. Where was it?

I rummaged frantically in my purse, but I already knew. I could see the key, exactly where I had put it so as not to forget it, on the little hall table right next to the door.

I looked at my driver, who stood waiting, a quizzical expression on her face. "I can't believe I've been so stupid, but I think I left the key at home. Do you know where the owners live? They might have another one they'd be willing to let me use . . ."

I trailed off as she shook her head. "This is just a holiday cottage. The Fergusons live in Inverness, I think. The postie would know."

It didn't matter, really, whether the postmaster had the Fergusons' address. If they weren't here on Iona, there was no practical way to get a key until tomorrow at the very earliest. Unless — "They wouldn't have given one to a neighbor, I suppose? In case of emergency? Or left one with the police?"

She tried to hide her amusement. "There are no police on Iona; we've no need of them. The nearest constable is on Mull, in Bunessen. And I doot they'd give a key to their property to anyone here on Iona; they've a poor opinion of islanders, have the Fergusons, and they're none so trusting. Ye can ask."

But her tone of voice told me the answer.

"No, you're probably right. I suppose I'll just have to find a hotel, or a B and B, if you have the time to take me around."

"Oh, I've the time, but I doot, this late in the season — the Argyll is full, I know. We passed it juist a few houses back, but they've a New Age group in for the week. Americans. And the St. Columba, up the hill, closed airly this year to be redone. Ye might try the Iona; it's new, and not so many people know about it."

"The Iona, then, by all means." The horse patiently turned the wagon in the narrow road, and we clopped back the way we had come, turning right when we neared the jetty to head up the hill toward the Abbey.

"That's the Nunnery we're passin'. I might as well give ye a bit of a tour while we're aboot it. It was built airly in the thirteenth century and flourished until the sixteenth, when all the nuns *and* monks were turned oot by the reformers. And round here, on your left, is the Heritage Centre. They've some fine wee bits and pieces to see, and if ye get hungry, walkin' aboot, they do lunch. Homemade soup and sandwiches, and homebaked sweets."

I was starved. I resolved to check out the Heritage Centre the moment I'd found a room for the night.

"That's the parish kirk next to the centre. Church of Scotland, ye know — Presbyterian, you Americans call it. Yon garden belongs to the St. Columba Hotel; they grow nearly all their own vegetables. *And* they run the wee shop across the road, there, books and woolens."

It sounded an odd combination, but appealing; I made another mental note.

"And here we are. Shall I wait for ye, in case they can't put ye up?"

"Oh, yes, please." I clambered down from my high perch, feeling stiff and stupid and every minute of my age.

The hotel was in what obviously had been a house, and a very large house for Iona. I knew that Iona used to be part of the Duke of Argyll's vast property, and assumed that the house had belonged to him or whoever he put in charge of the island. This would be, then, a miniature version of the "country house" hotels popular in England. I pushed open the great front door, petted the friendly gray tiger cat who lay on the counter, and rang the bell.

I was in luck. The pleasant woman who answered the bell had a charming face and a melodious, rather English-sounding voice; went to an English school, was my guess. She introduced her self as Hester Campbell and assured me that, yes, they could accommodate me; they had several rooms free, not large, but with en suite facilities (which, in Britspeak, meant a bathroom), if that would suit?

At that point a roomy closet would have been fine, so long as it had a bed. A private bath was an unexpected luxury. I gratefully signed the register and asked for my key.

"Key? Oh. Well — certainly there must be one somewhere — if you'd like me to look . . ." Mrs. Campbell had clearly never run into this particular eccentricity on the part of tourists, but was prepared to put herself out if I insisted. I smiled, accepted the idea that Iona was a place where police weren't needed and hotel rooms didn't have to be kept locked and, at my hostess's insistence, stepped into the lounge for a moment while she went out to deal with my bags.

There were seven people in the lounge, sitting in little silent clumps, and I recognized three of them. Teresa-not-of-Avila sat next to a very attractive young man with fair hair, dressed in a pale blue sweater and wearing one small gold earring. He shifted his feet uneasily and avoided looking at the nun. In a corner sat the two women from the bus, petulant expressions on both their faces. So they were staying on the island, were they? Well, perhaps I could avoid them.

A burly, bearded, sixtyish man in a sports jacket sat by himself, turning the pages of a magazine, and a very thin, pale young man with big, awkward hands and bad skin sat in front of the fireplace next to a strikingly lovely silver-haired woman in her fifties, both of them staring into space. As they became aware of me, every face turned in my direction, and every one of them wore the same expression.

Surely it was my imagination that all these strangers looked at me with naked hostility.

2

Alan Nesbitt tells me I have sound instincts, and should pay more attention to them. I will regret for the rest of my life that I did not heed my instinct then and leave Iona by the next ferry.

In any event, I told myself I was imagining things, turned away from the unwelcoming faces, and dismissed the matter. I went out to pay my obliging driver and book a full tour of the island for the next morning, took possession of my room, and unpacked (with the aid of the cat, who was introduced as Stan and who found it necessary to sniff every article of my luggage). A quick glance in the mirror told me I looked neat, at least, which at sixty-something is often all that can be expected, so I pulled my hat to a little more rakish angle, smiled at myself, and hied off to the Heritage Centre before they stopped serving lunch.

The lunchroom was a tiny room at one side of the museum; if the building had originally been the manse for the parish kirk next door, as seemed likely, this might have been a spare bedroom. The ambience was amateurish, with a distinct aura of church basement, but the thick soup was warming and delicious, the sandwiches were made of crusty homemade bread, and the woman serving me, the last customer of the day, was friendly. A short, plump, cheerful woman wrapped in a businesslike apron, she bustled about clearing tables and putting things away in the minute kitchen, chatting all the while. Finally finished with her chores, she poured herself the last cup of coffee and sat down to share the last two brownies with me.

"This was just what I needed," I said with a contented sigh. "I'm Dorothy Martin, by the way."

"Maggie McIntyre. And what brought ye to Iona so late in the year?"

I explained about my friends and the plans that had gone wrong. "But you're the second person to mention it being late. I would have thought September —"

"Late for here. The storms will be comin' soon, now. There's no' a trace o' land from here to Newfoundland, ye see, and the winds can get a wee bit strong when they've that many miles of sea to cross."

"I can well imagine. Hurricanes, do you mean?"

"No' hurricanes, quite, but gales, wi' rain, an' thunder. The seas rise, an' ye canna see yer hand before yer face, it's that dark. And wi' no warnin', oot of a clear, blue sky, as they say."

I glanced out of the window at the clear, blue sky and the leaves moving lazily in the gentle breeze, and Maggie chuckled.

"No, ye've no need to worry today. It'll be a week or two, likely, before they start, though ye never know. But that's why the tourist season here ends at the beginning of October. I mind one year, when the storms began airly, there was a couple oot in a dinghy. Germans, they were, good people, wi' a pair o' bairns waitin' behind." She sighed and paused, remembering, and then finished her coffee and stood up briskly. " 'Twas the next mornin' before the Coastguard could get their helicopters oot to search. The boat had fetched up on Ardnamurchan, twenty, twenty-five miles northeast o' here. He was still alive, but they never found her. I canna offer ye more coffee, for I've drunk the last drop, but I'd be happy to make ye a cup of tea?"

I can take a hint as well as anybody, and the gorgeous afternoon was beckoning. "No, thanks, but I'll be back tomorrow, I expect. So nice to meet you, and we'll hope the storms don't come early this year."

I put the sad little story out of my mind and went exploring. The Heritage Centre itself I would save for another day; it was inside and I wanted to be out, out in the sunshine, out in the air that was reviving me with every breath. I wandered across the road to the very lovely ruins of the Nunnery.

It may sound odd to refer to ruins as lovely, but the soft pink granite of the broken walls glowed in the afternoon sun, and the few arches that still remained had lost none of their delicate beauty. A well-tended garden nodded gently in what might have been the old cloister, and here and there tiny plants bloomed cheerfully in niches of the walls. I sat on a bench in the sun and watched as small birds flitted in and out of the empty windows or perched atop roofless walls. Bees and butterflies and large, beautiful dragonflies roamed among the flowers, and in one sunny corner a small black-and-white cat sat washing itself, now and then pausing, one paw in the air, to eye the birds. The Nunnery was, in its gentle way, a busy place, but utterly peaceful.

I sat, drowsily trying to analyze the quiet. It wasn't an absence of sound, exactly. I could hear the beat of wings when a bird flew overhead, the clop of a horse's hooves as one of the wagons went down the village street. Somewhere people laughed, and a dog barked.

It wasn't until an ancient tractor chugged noisily past the Nunnery that I put my finger on it. There was, except for the odd car or farm vehicle, no traffic noise on Iona. I knew that residents could bring cars onto the island, but they seemed to use them mostly between home and the ferry landing. Otherwise, everyone cycled or walked, so the loudest noises were natural ones, and the occasional toot of the ferry.

I stretched luxuriously in the sun. I could get used to this.

However, I realized shortly, I could also get what my grandmother used to call "the dead sets" if I didn't move soon. I rose reluctantly and headed on down to the village.

The shop displaying Scottish crafts drew me, but I resisted temptation and went instead to the jetty, the heart of the village. Perching on a post, I watched for a while. The little ferry plied tirelessly back and forth, each time taking a few passengers and bringing a few back. On one trip a garbage truck, looking very much out of place, lumbered off the boat and groaned its way down the village street, emptying trash bins with the usual hideous noises.

That did it. Romance lay elsewhere. I puffed back up the hill and was about to turn in at my hotel when a church bell began to ring. The Abbey, I assumed from the direction, and I hadn't been there yet. Partly from a sense of having transgressed against proper tourist etiquette, and partly because I find church bells irresistible, I panted another few yards uphill and joined the last few stragglers walking into the church.

The service, to an Episcopalian used to a fixed liturgy, was pleasant but rather odd. It seemed to follow no particular pattern, but there were hymns and readings, some of them poetry, some from the scriptures of various religious traditions, and prayers of the sort that are designed not to offend anyone. Well, I already knew that the Iona Community, which was in charge of the Abbey, was a nondenominational group, so I hadn't exactly expected Evensong.

When someone — a lay person, I gathered from the absence of vestments — launched into a rather rambling sermon, my mind and eyes began to wander. I was a little disappointed in the Abbey, I decided. Though lofty and attractive enough, it held none of that sense of antiquity I had come to expect in British churches. After all, there had been a church of some kind on this spot since

563! Of course, I reminded myself, the present building, though begun in the twelfth century, had fallen to ruins by the sixteenth, and the "restoration" completed some thirty or forty years ago had really amounted to an almost total rebuilding. So perhaps it was little wonder that the ghosts of past worshipers seemed to have departed.

Worshipers. My eyes roved over the present congregation. There were a lot of earnest-looking young people in blue jeans, part of an Iona Community retreat or some such, I surmised. The small group in garments that tended to flow were probably the New Agers from the Argyll Hotel that my guide had mentioned. And the group right in front of me, seven of them stretched out in one pew — I sighed. There was Teresa, and the pair from the bus, and the rest as well.

On a small island, it was going to be hard to avoid the unfriendly crew from the Iona Hotel.

I sneaked out before the service was quite over so as to escape them, and wandered around the Abbey grounds, looking at the lovely old Celtic crosses and the graves of, among others, one MacBeth. It was while I was wondering about him — surely he couldn't be the original of the story Shake-

31

speare made immortal? — that the little hotel group came out of the church, somewhat apart from the rest of the congregation, and assembled in front of the largest cross. I watched from my vantage point in the churchyard as a clergywoman from the Abbey joined them.

It appeared that she was giving them a little speech of welcome. The fitful wind caught her words and flung them at me now and again. "Iona Community delighted and honored . . . seven such stalwart laborers in God's vineyard . . . wish you joy and peace here . . . let us pray."

I didn't stay for the prayer. The wind was getting cold as twilight closed in, and besides, I was bemused. Laborers in God's vineyard? That antagonistic bunch? It takes all kinds, certainly, and maybe I'd misjudged them, but . . . I climbed up the steps to the hotel and went to my room to put on warmer clothes and speculate about personalities.

Dinner was included in the price of my room, and from the aromas wafting up the stairs, it was going to be delicious. I debated about going down to the lounge for an aperitif, but decided against it. I'd be better able to face unfriendly people with some food inside me, and in any case, I had a couple of phone calls to make. There was no phone in the room; I collected some change and went downstairs to the pay phone in the hall.

The first call was to Lynn.

"Oh, *good,* you're there. We tried to call you earlier, but you must have been out doing the island. Isn't the cottage *delightful?*"

I sighed and explained. Lynn's silver peal of laughter sparkled across the miles.

"It *thrills* me when other people do things like that. I can't wait to tell Tom; he'll *adore* it."

"And how is Tom?"

Tom was at home, asleep at the moment, and doing much better, though chafing under diet restrictions, Lynn reported. They hadn't had to do any bypass surgery or angioplasty or anything, and his doctor had told him he could travel in another few days if he wanted to.

"Well, when he gets up here to crab and salmon-land, he won't mind low-fat eating. Soon, I hope?"

"This weekend, if all goes well. But I'll call."

So I gave her the hotel number, just in case it took me forever to recapture the lost key, and went on to the next call.

"Jane? I'm so glad you're home . . . yes,

I've arrived, and it really is a lovely place . . . yes, well, that's why I called. I don't know how the cottage is; I've done a really stupid thing."

I explained about the key. "Apparently, there isn't another one closer than Inverness, and what with the ferries and all, that's a couple of days' journey from here. We really are in the middle of nowhere, which is one of the things that make it so nice, but right now I wish civilization were a little closer. Anyway, do you think you could mail me the key? How long do you think it would take to get here?"

Jane's dry voice came over the line quite clearly. "Any place else, I'd say a day, but you're back of beyond, there. You'd best count on two. I'll go and post it straight off. You having a good time?"

"Well — yes, on the whole. There are some rather odd people here at the hotel, but I'll only be here another day or two, so I won't have to mix with them much. I'm getting a lot of exercise, and I do love the island. It's just as peaceful as everybody says. How's my house, and how are the cats?"

"What you'd expect. House looking a total disaster but coming along, cats missing you but bearing up."

"I miss them, too, but there's a nice cat

here at the hotel." Stan was at the moment twining himself, purring, around my ankles. I reached down and petted him; his purr stepped up to fortissimo. "Any news?"

"Alan rang up."

"Oh?" My heart beat a little faster despite my stern inner admonition not to be silly.

"Wants your phone number when you have one. He'll ring again. What shall I tell him?"

"I hardly know. I'd call him, but there's only a pay phone, and all the way to Brussels — look, I'll give you the number of the hotel so he can reach me if he has to, but tell him I'm fine, really, and I'll call him when I move into the cottage." I read her the number, and hung up feeling lonesome.

The rest of the guests were already seated when I walked into the dining room. It looked as though the seven other guests and I had the hotel to ourselves. They were seated in the same pairings I had observed earlier, and seemed just about as cordial. The man with the beard was again alone, and on impulse I stopped the waiter as he was about to lead me to my table for one.

"Wait a minute. I hate to dine alone." I approached the bearded man. "I see you're by yourself, and I am, too. Would you mind sharing a table?"

One of the advantages of age is that one can make a suggestion like that without being suspected of ulterior motives. The man looked a little startled, but gestured to the other chair. "Please." He even stood up, a nice little courtesy most males have abandoned.

I chose barley soup over a cold appetizer and ordered a bottle of bordeaux to go with the roast beef. "I hope you'll share it with me?"

The bearded face split in a grin, and the appealing brown eyes lost their sad look for a moment. "If you let me buy the next bottle. You're staying a few days, yes?"

"I'm not quite sure, actually. I'll be on the island for a couple of weeks, but I'm moving to a cottage in a day or two." By the time we'd finished our soup he knew the whole story of Tom's medical problems and my lost key. "My name's Dorothy Martin, by the way, and even though I live in England, you can tell from my accent that I'm American. I gather you are, too?"

"Jake Goldstein, Chicago." He inclined his head in a semibow.

"Are the seven of you traveling together?" I encompassed the room with my eyes as the waiter set plates in front of us.

His eyes rose emphatically to heaven.

"Together! You could say together, if you mean we go the same places at the same time. Me, I'm just along for the ride."

Well, that didn't tell me much. I tried again. "Is it some sort of tour, or something?"

He sighed and took a good-sized gulp of wine. "Or something. To tell you the truth, Mrs. Martin —"

"Dorothy."

"— Dorothy, I'd be better off at home. I should've known better, but —" He raised his shoulders and his hands in an elaborate shrug. "So I like salmon. So is that enough that I should have to put up with a bunch of — look, I'll tell you the whole story." He glanced around the room and lowered his voice.

"Like I said, I'm from Chicago. So there's this organization, see, the Chicago Religious Assembly. You've heard maybe of the National Religious Assembly?"

I nodded. The ecumenical group was well-known throughout the United States.

"Yeah, well, the Chicago branch has money to burn. So they decide to have this contest. All the big religious groups are supposed to pick one person who's done the most, for the congregation or the neighborhood or whatever. And then the assembly chooses the biggest seven of all and sends us all on this two-week trip to Scotland."

"I see." I did see. Seven people, all from different religious backgrounds, all stalwarts of their own faith, possibly even zealots. "It sounds," I said, feeling my way cautiously, "like the sort of thing that could — um — generate ill feeling unless it were handled very tactfully."

"Ill feeling!" Jake shrugged again, and once more rolled his eyes to the ceiling. "Listen, a mushroom cloud should appear tomorrow over Iona, you'll know why. We've been together for a week, now. Edinburgh, Inverness, Glasgow — long enough for them all to decide they hate each other. Me, I'm an outsider. The Quaker got appendicitis at the last minute and they got me to come so they shouldn't waste a ticket. I ask you, a rabbi ending up on Iona! It was a free vacation, so I'm here, and sometimes I try to keep the peace, but better you should get into a fight between two alley cats than some of these Christians!"

" 'See how these Christians love one another'?" I quoted.

"You got it."

We ate in silence for a few minutes, and then I replenished both our wineglasses. "I confess I'm intrigued. I've met one of your party, Sister — er, that is, Teresa. Can you tell me about the others?"

"So we've eaten our dinner, and I won't spoil my appetite. So. Five others." He ticked them off on his fingers. "Hattie Mae Brown. She's black. Baptist. Leads her church choir."

I could just see her swaying in a gold lamé choir robe, having a wonderful time.

"Janet Douglas. Presbyterian. Gardener."

"Gardener? But —"

"Does church gardens all over Chicago. Works of art." His dry tone left me in doubt as to whether he considered the work to be of great value or not. He went on with his list, touching his middle finger. "Grace Desmond. Unitarian. Feeds the hungry."

"That sounds worthwhile."

Take just grunted and went on with his list. "Bob Williams. Methodist." He was the ring finger. "Youth leader. Big church, works with neighborhood kids, too. And Chris Olafson's Lutheran, big-shot organist. "

He might well have been the one the two women had been discussing on the bus, then. I've known a good many gay musicians, especially, for some reason, organists.

"Toffee pudding?" asked our young waiter, approaching with a tray. "Or cheese? Or both?"

"Pudding for me," I said. Jake nodded.

"Coffee's served in the lounge," the waiter said as he put down our desserts. "And here's cream for your pudding, unless you'd rather have custard?"

"Cream is lovely, thanks." I poured it greedily, golden richness so thick it almost needed to be spooned, and offered the pitcher to Jake. He shook his head regretfully.

"I touch that stuff, my doctor has a heart attack even before I do."

I thought about Tom Anderson coming to all this forbidden bounty, and then shrugged. Lynn and I would be doing his cooking, and we'd avoid the cholesterol. Meanwhile I'd enjoy it and worry about the consequences later (a decision I make with regrettable frequency).

"Now," I said when I'd eaten about half the sticky, rich, sinful, incredibly good mixture, "tell me what they all have against me."

Jake raised his bushy black eyebrows.

"When I walked into the lounge before lunch, you were all sitting there, and everyone looked daggers at me. Even you."

"Oh. Yeah. No, that was just general ill will, had nothing to do with you. Except — I don't know." He tilted his head to one side and pulled at an earlobe. "Now you mention it, you might be a problem. A catalyst, see what I mean?"

"No," I said flatly.

"Tell you what. Bring the rest of your pudding, have some coffee with me, and you'll see for yourself."

I didn't know what Jake was talking about, but curiosity is my besetting sin, and Iona seemed likely to provide few other amusements after nightfall, so I followed Jake into the lounge and sat down in one of the plush armchairs while he went to the sideboard to get us both some coffee.

Stan had obviously sized me up as a soft touch. I had barely sat down before he was in my lap, inquiring about the cream on my pudding.

"Wait till I've finished," I whispered conspiratorially. "I'll let you lick the bowl. We won't tell your people." Although it was apparent, from his behavior, that Stan operated under very few inconvenient rules.

As I waited for Jake and the coffee, I glanced casually around the room, trying to establish what sociologists call the "group dynamic." The trouble was that, as far as I could tell, there wasn't any group dynamic, because what I was looking at wasn't a group. It was a collection of individuals. The only people who were sitting together were the tall young man with bad skin and the elegant silver-haired woman, and as I watched out of the corner of my eye, she said something brief, stood up, and walked away, while his face turned even paler than usual and his hands clenched. I was the only one who saw the little scene; the other four people, sitting separated from each other, were concentrating very hard on their coffee. No one spoke.

Jake handed me a cup of coffee and sat down. I finished my pudding and put the bowl on the floor, rattling the spoon a bit. I hoped the noise would cover my muttered "Tell me which is which."

"We can't whisper," he muttered back, stirring his coffee longer than necessary. "They'll think we're plotting something."

"Then introduce me."

Jake rolled his eyes heavenward. On the whole I agreed with him; I'd probably regret this. But there are times when my curiosity outweighs my caution, and really, how much unpleasantness could I get into in a day or two?

"It's your funeral." Jake stood up. "Hey, everybody! I want you to meet Dorothy Martin, here, a fellow American. I've told her about our trip, and she wanted to get to know you. Teresa I guess you've already met, huh?"

I smiled at Teresa; she nodded and returned her eyes to her coffee.

"And this is our Grace — Grace Desmond." He indicated the beautiful woman still standing at the sideboard. She came over and held out a correct, if not cordial, hand.

"What an appropriate name," I said. "You look so much like Grace Kelly."

"How do you do, Mrs. Martin," she replied coldly, clasped my hand for the minimum possible time, and turned her back. I caught a glint of amusement in Jake's eye.

"Janet Douglas is hiding over there in the corner, and that's Hattie Mae Brown on the couch."

"Janet, Hattie Mae." Janet was the wiry little woman Hattie Mae had been talking to on the bus, but they weren't talking now. Janet glanced up and then looked away without so much as a nod; Hattie Mae smiled doubtfully, glanced from Jake to me, and said, "Pleased to meetcha," before turning back to the magazine she was pretending to read.

"And the gentlemen are Chris Olafson —" he indicated the good-looking blond in the blue sweater, who nodded without enthusiasm "— and Bob Williams."

Bob unfolded his length from the squishy

armchair and stood. He walked over to me with the corners of his mouth turned resolutely up and his hand extended.

"You are welcome among us, Mrs. Martin," he said in the kind of hushed, pious voice that makes my toes curl. "I don't know where you live in America, or if you have a church home, but —"

"Actually, I live in England now. How do you do, Mr. Williams." I took his hand and then tried not to wipe mine on my slacks.

"It's a pleasure to meet you," I said brightly and untruthfully to the room in general. "I'll only be staying in the hotel for a night or two, but perhaps we'll see each other walking around the island. I'm sure you'll excuse me if I make an early night of it, after a long journey, and I hope you all have a wonderful time on Iona."

Before I escaped to my room, I thought I heard from Hattie Mae a loud, skeptical "Hmmph!"

3

In the small hours of the night the wind began to rise. A tree branch scraped against my window, my curtains flapped. The sounds crept into my dreams, creating images of a creaky ship, sailing hell-for-leather to an unknown but dreaded destination. When an especially loud crack of the sails finally woke me, I lay tense, my heart pounding, wondering if it had been a real sound or mere nightmare terror. I could hear nothing but the tumult of the wind, and gradually I relaxed, told myself it had been a gust slamming a door shut, put in my earplugs, and slept dreamlessly for the rest of the night.

In the morning, night terrors were forgotten. Brilliant sunshine left no dark corners for them to lurk in, and the sounds of the diminished wind were gentle and soothing. The weather had changed, though; it was cold in the room. I shivered when I finally crawled out from under my duvet and banged the window shut. Bless Lynn for warning me about the weather! I pulled out my warmest slacks and sweater, and debated a while before leaving the long underwear in the drawer.

Once I was dressed and warm, I made some tea with the electric kettle in the room, and sat down to consider last night's uncomfortable little scene in the lounge.

Through bad luck and my own stupidity, I'd landed in the middle of a group of people who were antagonistic toward each other and, apparently, toward me as well — except for Jake, who was pleasant enough. Now, there are people who seem to thrive on conflict, but I'm not one of them. I'm more comfortable with harmony and goodwill, and it was pretty obvious there wasn't a lot of that in this crowd. And I'd seen what Jake meant about a catalyst. Tensions were ready to boil up. If one of them decided I made a convenient scapegoat, an excuse for a quarrel — or, on the other hand, if one confided in me, invited me to take sides — well, either way, I'd end up in the middle in more than one sense.

So I'd better steer clear of them. It ought to be easy enough to do. Mealtimes were the risky times, but with a little planning I could surely hit the dining room when the rest were all ready to leave. Look preoccupied, take a book, and stick to my table for one. I had fallen in love with Iona already, and I

46

wasn't going to let a bunch of strangers spoil it for me. A pity about Jake — I'd have enjoyed getting to know him — but maybe I'd have a chance later in the week, away from the hotel.

With which sensible resolution I looked at the clock (late enough, surely), picked up a mystery novel I'd brought with me, and went in search of breakfast. The stairway, a carefully preserved remnant of the fine house this used to be, was built in a lovely curve, with beautifully carved balusters; I lifted my head and became the Duchess of Argyll on the way down. The impersonation suffered when I tripped over Stan, who was napping in a sunny patch at the foot of the stairs. He moved off with a reproachful yowl, and I, plain Dorothy Martin again, went in to get my breakfast.

The dining room was a cheery place in the morning, with strong sunshine pouring in through the east windows. I had timed it almost right; Hattie Mae was sitting at a table in the corner. She looked up when I came in and gestured with her coffee cup. I smiled distantly and headed for a table on the other side of the room.

I was allowed to order in peace, and had gotten halfway through my kipper and eggs before a shadow fell across the book I had propped in front of my plate. I looked up, reluctantly; Hattie Mae's bulk stood between me and the sunlight.

"What you readin'?"

"*What Mrs. McGillicuddy Saw.* It's an old Agatha Christie, one of my favorites." Whoops, tactical mistake. I had admitted I'd read the book before. It's a little hard to pretend you're totally engrossed in a book you know like the back of your hand.

Hattie Mae was sharp. "Oh, then I ain't stoppin' you from knowin' who done it. Mind if I sit down?"

Well, what could I do, short of being totally rude to the woman? I waved my hand at the other chair and took a bite of kipper. If my mouth was full she couldn't expect me to carry on a conversation.

But Hattie Mae was perfectly capable of keeping things going all by herself.

"I just thought I ought to warn you to be careful, honey. You seem like a nice woman, and there's a lot of funny people around here. You got to take care of yourself among the godless. 'Be sober, be vigilant; because your adversary the devil, as a roaring lion, walketh about, seeking whom he may devour.' First Peter 5:8."

I swallowed a kipper bone the wrong way and had a coughing fit, and by the time

Hattie Mae had finished pounding me on the back she was feeling protective, and ready for a good, long chat.

"Now, Dottie," she began eagerly.

"Dorothy," I said, as firmly as I could in my choked voice. " 'Dottie' is an insult on this side of the Atlantic."

"Okay, Dorothy!" Hattie Mae beamed. "My, I'm glad you told me, honey! Now listen, we don't got much time, and I wanted to be *sure* you knew what all was goin' on here, before it's too late."

"Actually, I don't think —"

"I tell you, Dottie — Dorothy — if I'd a knowed what kind of people I'd have to be travelin' with, I'd a never came on this here trip!" She leaned over the table, her ample bosom just missing my book, and began to hiss at me in a kind of stage whisper — entirely unnecessarily, since we were alone in the room. "I ain't never seen such a scandalous bunch o' folks callin' theirselves Christians! 'For such are false apostles, deceitful workers, transforming themselves into the apostles of Christ.' Second Corinthians 11:13."

I was ready for that one; I was eating eggs. Safer.

"Why, did you know, that Jake you was talkin' to last night ain't even a Christian at

49

all, but a Jew! An' that Grace, she's a Unitarian, and that's just as bad; they don't believe nothin', s' far as I can make out. Bob, he thinks he's the only one among us that's got religion, and he never shuts up about it. He's at least a Methodist, an' that's respectable. But that nun! Would you believe it? A nun, carryin' on in blue jeans and a T-shirt! An' I don't trust them Cath'lics, nohow. That Janet, she ain't got too good a temper, and she don't think much of me, neither, 'cause I'm black and I know my Bible better than she does. But the worst of 'em all is that — that —" She shuddered and took a sip of my water to fortify herself, and I took advantage of the brief lull.

"If you're referring to Mr. Olafson, I believe he's a very fine musician, you know. I understand you're a musician, yourself. Perhaps one day the two of you could give us a concert."

I got my own back, anyway. It was Hattie Mae's turn to choke. Coughing, chins wobbling, she put down the glass and glared at me.

"Dorothy, I don't think you understand what I'm tryin' to tell you," Hattie Mae began when she was able to speak. "That man is one of Those! He —"

I put my fork down. My food didn't taste

quite so good anymore. "Hattie Mae. What I understand is that you've taken a dislike to your fellow travelers. They may not all be appealing people, but I wish you'd let me make up my own mind about them. I don't like to prejudge people. Now if you'll excuse me, I have an appointment."

"Well! I was just tryin' to warn you! But suit yourself!"

Her voice followed me out the dining room door and into the hall, where I pulled my jacket from its peg, jammed on my hat, and made for the front door.

"Excuse me!" Teresa sounded as put out as she had every right to be; I had run smack into her. She was standing in front of the door with Stan in her arms, or he had been; she sucked at a scratch on her hand as she glared at me.

"Sorry," I muttered and pushed past her to the front stairs, taking in deep lungfuls of the good, clean air as I walked down the steps.

The driver of the horse-drawn wagon was waiting in front of the hotel. "Beautiful morning," she greeted me.

"Beautiful. 'Where every prospect pleases, and only man is vile.'" She looked politely inquiring. "A hymn. Never mind. By the way, my name's Dorothy Martin. I feel silly not knowing yours."

"Deirdre Cameron." She helped me up and clucked to her horse. "I'm very happy to meet ye, Mrs. Martin."

In her soft voice, with the delightfully trilled *r*s, the standard courtesy somehow sounded sincere.

"Now we're passin' the Abbey, as of course ye know. The Celtic crosses ye see are not the originals. Those were nearly all destroyed by the reformers, and the few that were spared had weathered so badly by the twentieth century that the Iona Trust put them in the Abbey Museum, to be protected, and erected the copies ye see here. The biggest one is St. Martin's cross . . ."

We went on our peaceful way toward the north end of the island, passing Bob on the way. I ducked, like the coward I am. I had no intention of offering him a ride and being preached at all morning; I'd had enough of that already. When we had gone as far as the road would take us, we turned back down the hill, past the Abbey and through the village. The sun had warmed the air and colored the sea a dazzling aquamarine.

"What's that boat that's going out, Deirdre? The one you can barely see, heading north?"

"That's the *Iolaire*, Davie MacPherson's boat. He takes it to Staffa every morning and afternoon when the weather's good. Do ye know Staffa?"

"Only by reputation. It's the island Mendelssohn liked so much, isn't it? The one the *Fingal's Cave* overture is written about?"

"That's right. Ye must take the trip; it's one of the things tourists to Iona are obliged to do."

I laughed, and we headed on to the south, passing the tiny grocery store, where I saw Jake coming out with a loaded bag. And after that dinner we'd had!

On the south end of the island, the road turned west before petering out to a track. Deirdre pulled her horse to a stop and pointed.

"Ye'll want to walk on to Columba's Bay one day, but mind ye dinna go alone. The path is marshy, and it's easy to turn an ankle on the rocks. And if ye get lost, ye could find yourself at the marble quarry, and that can be dangerous."

"Marble is quarried on Iona? I didn't realize there was any industry here at all."

"Och, no, not for years now, not since 1915 or so. It's fine marble, mind ye, and there's Iona greenstone as well — granite, that is — but most of the buyers in the old days were in Belgium, and the first war shut down the trade. Somehow it's never started again, but some of the machinery's still there, great rusting hulks, and slabs of marble they never bothered to take away." She shuddered a little. "I dinna like the place myself — the only ugly bit of Iona, to my way of thinking. God made this island, and he's everywhere on it — 'tis a holy place, Iona." She said it very simply. "But not the quarry. Man took that and ruined it, and I'm thinking the devil himself owns that bit." She clucked again to her horse, and we set off back to the hotel.

I would certainly stay away from the quarry. The peace of Iona had possessed me during my lovely morning, and I was resolved to hold on to it. Even, I thought as I went into the hotel to change into cooler clothes, in the face of the Chicago crowd.

Since my terms at the hotel didn't include lunch, I went again to the Heritage Centre's little lunchroom and talked to Maggie, after the crowd had cleared out.

"And have ye been enjoying yourself, then?"

"Do you know the story of the curate's egg?" I answered. She shook her head. "A curate was breakfasting with his bishop, and was served a boiled egg that wasn't very fresh, to put it mildly. When the bishop asked him if he'd enjoyed his egg, the curate replied, 'Thank you, my lord. Parts of it were excellent.' "

Maggie laughed. "Which parts are which?"

"I love the island itself, and the islanders I've met — you, and Deirdre who drives the wagon, and Hester up at the hotel. But there are some Americans staying at the hotel who — well, they don't get along, and one of them seems determined to draw me into their quarrels, and that isn't so pleasant. I'm trying to keep out of their way."

"Why don't ye go off to Staffa this afternoon?" Maggie suggested. "It could well be your last chance for days. Ye know we talked about our storms? Well, dear, the barometer's falling. We'll get a storm by morning, is my prediction. And this time of year ye never know how bad they'll be, nor how long they'll last."

"But I'm here for two weeks!"

"Ye never know," she repeated. "If David is takin' the boat oot this afternoon, ye can be sure it's safe. And it's a good day for it; the basalt will be good and dry, with all the wind. It can be slippery to walk on when it's wet. Ye must suit yourself, of course, but in your place I'd go. It's not to be missed, ye know. Are ye a good sailor?"

"Not especially, to tell the truth. And I

didn't think to bring along any motion sickness pills."

"Then go to the shop in the village and get some of the ginger capsules. Much better for ye than drugs; they won't put ye to sleep, and they'll do the job."

I was ready for a walk anyway, so I wandered down to the village, lingering to gaze at the tiny village school, Dr. Kate McIntosh's office (hours in Bunessen Tuesday and Thursday afternoons, Iona Wednesday mornings only), and the notice board by the public telephones, advertising the bus and ferry schedules, lost kittens, and a *ceilidh* Friday evening in the village hall. I would have to find out from someone what a *ceilidh* was — and, for that matter, how to pronounce it!

The little shop, a general store that stocked everything from souvenirs to needlepoint kits, was having a sale on the ginger capsules, so I bought several boxes. If they were as good as Maggie said, I could use them on the ferries going back home, and in planes, though I still hadn't made up my mind about Staffa this afternoon.

I turned back as I was leaving the shop. "Oh, by the way, what's a sea-lid?"

The clerk looked blank.

"It said on the notice board that there was

56

going to be one Friday, in the village hall. C-e-i-l-something."

"Och, a kay-lee!"

My mind tried to reconcile the spelling with the pronunciation, and gave up. "It's Gaelic, I suppose?"

"Aye. Dinna ye know aboot *ceilidhs?* It's a dance party. They'll do traditional dancing to begin, and then when the young ones show up, it'll be rock. Ye must come; it's great fun. We'll teach ye the dances!"

"I'll be there." I was smiling as I walked back up the road.

I lingered on the jetty for a while. The place had captured my imagination. To a landlubber, there is something about boats and nets and seagulls and the smell of salt air that is deeply invigorating. Today the sea threw back diamond glints of hard, bright sunlight, and the wind caught the sails of the little boats on the Sound and sent them flying like the gulls. It was so beautiful I could hardly bear it.

And there, bobbing gently at her mooring, was the *Iolaire*, the Staffa boat, brightly painted and inviting.

A gull swooped down next to me, thinking that someone who sat so still must surely have some crumbs worth considering. When it saw that I hadn't, it gave a jeering cry and flew away, and the other gulls joined its cries in a raucous, enticing nautical chorus.

I went back to the hotel for my waterproof jacket.

I didn't forget, though, to ask at the desk if there was any mail. If a miracle had happened, my key might have arrived.

This wasn't my day for miracles. I was going to have to spend one more day with the other unfriendly guests. Ah, well, doubtless there were worse fates, but I was glad to be getting away from them for the afternoon.

I was the first to board the *Iolaire* for the afternoon sailing. I swallowed two of the ginger capsules, hoping for the best, and took a seat in the bow where I could see everything.

What I saw, when I'd finished inspecting the boat and a portion of the beach, was the Chicago contingent, trooping down the street straight for the jetty.

Of course! I should have known. They were only here for the week, and they would have heard the same warnings I had about the weather. Of course they would want to make sure they saw Staffa. And to tell the truth, there wasn't a great deal to do on Iona anyway. It was a place to relax and unwind, to appreciate the rather savage beauties of nature, but if you were at odds with your fellow travelers, a trip off the island must seem like a very good idea.

Look at me, after all — running away from them.

In the minute or so it took them to reach the boat I gave myself a stern talking-to. Pull yourself together, Dorothy, old girl. This is *not* your usual form. Whatever possessed you, refusing to face a problem? Not even a problem, merely a small unpleasantness. I'm ashamed of you!

I'm here to have a good time, not put up with a bunch of creeps, my baser self whined.

And you think the way to enjoy yourself is to cut yourself off from your fellow man? Fellow Americans, at that!

I don't like them.

And how do you know? You've had ten minutes' conversation with them, if that. All except for Jake, and you like him well enough. Hattie Mae is tough to take, true, but she's a Christian, you're a Christian — there ought to be some common meeting ground.

Yes, but ...

But nothing. Stand up, look them in the eye, and smile. Even if they're mad at each other, there's no reason for you to be disagreeable to them.

I stood up, staggering a little as the boat rose to an incoming swell, smiled brilliantly at the group, and waved.

Jake, first to board, nodded slightly, then turned to give Grace a hand. She didn't even glance my way. One by one they stepped over the gunwale. Hattie Mae glared; so did Teresa. Bob seemed moody and Chris preoccupied; Janet pursed her lips and looked away. They settled themselves in various areas of the boat, well separated from one another, and from me.

I sat down again. So much for that. It would, I assured myself furiously, be a hot day in Siberia before I so much as spoke to any of them again. No wonder they didn't enjoy traveling together. What was wrong with them, anyway?

That thought occupied me while a handful of other passengers boarded and we pulled away from the jetty. I couldn't escape the odd feeling that there were undercurrents I didn't know about. These people seemed disturbed at a level that couldn't be explained simply by ill temper, or even religious antagonism. It felt as though there were strong personal animosities involved, but how could that be, among a group that knew each other only casually?

I watched them covertly as the *Iolaire* crossed the Sound to Fionnphort, picked up a few more passengers, and headed out to sea. Bob sat in the bow, well away from the others, looking sulky and miserable. Jake, seated on a sort of metal box in the middle of the deck, had his back to me, so I couldn't see his expression, but he certainly wasn't enjoying the scenery; his view consisted of the inside of the passenger cabin. Most of the group were in there, somewhat hidden from me; I could see only that they were neither talking to each other nor looking out the windows.

Clearly, something was wrong. Equally clearly, it was none of my business. I washed my hands of them and concentrated on enjoying myself.

The ginger capsules, spreading a gentle warmth through my insides, made the motion of the boat actually pleasant, like being rocked in a rather unpredictable cradle. And the view was spectacular. There were seals along the way, sunning themselves on a rock, and birds — gulls, of course, and cormorants, and others I didn't recognize. The sea was high enough to make me glad of my waterproof jacket; spray leapt into the bow every time we hit an especially big wave. When we came near a tiny outcropping of rock and the skipper slowed the boat so we could all see the comical, colorful birds called puffins, I stood up and risked being swept overboard while I madly took pictures.

The Chicagoans, when I sneaked a glance into the cabin, weren't doing so well. Now and then, when the wind changed direction for a moment, I could hear muffled groans. Well, they'd doubtless be all right, and at least they were feeling too rotten to bother me, which made it easier to leave them strictly alone.

However, when Grace Desmond staggered out on deck, pea green, and took a precautionary seat at the rail, my conscience began to smite me. I argued with myself for a moment or two, then made my way over to her, swaying and staggering myself as the boat rose and dipped.

"Look, can you take pills without water? I have the most marvelous seasick preventives. I don't know if they'll cure it, but surely it's worth a try. They're not drugs, just ginger and chamomile. Here." I handed her the bubble pack.

"I have water." It was one of the passengers from Mull, looking sympathetic. He took a plastic bottle from his backpack and handed it to Grace. She was too miserable even to thank him, but punched out a couple of capsules, swallowed them with a swig, and leaned back, looking as if she'd like to die. I bravely went into the cabin.

"I have some capsules for motion sickness, if anyone's interested."

I might have been giving away twenty-dollar bills. Some of them even tried to pay me, but I waved their money away. "Take up a collection back at the hotel, if they really help. Or buy some in the village and replenish my supply. And you'd be better off out on deck, you know. The fresh air helps a lot, even if you do get a bit wet."

It was Teresa who produced the water this time and handed it round. Feeling like Florence Nightingale, I went back on deck and sat down on the starboard side to watch the slow approach of Staffa.

4

The approach was slow, indeed. When the skipper's son appeared briefly on deck to perform some mysterious sailorly rite, I asked him how much longer we'd be.

"Three quarters of an hour. The current's slowing us a bit, this trip."

Forty-five minutes is a good deal of time for a sociable person like me to go without talking, and I hadn't thought to bring anything to read. The view by this time was somewhat boring: sea, and more sea, and sky, and, in the distance, the blue-gray outline of Staffa, at this distance looking not much different from the surrounding water.

So I actually smiled, if cautiously, when Grace sat down by my side.

"I hope you're feeling better."

"Much better. I owe you profound thanks."

"No problem. I'm glad the ginger did the trick."

"Mrs. Martin —"

"Dorothy, please."

"Dorothy, then, I feel I must apologize for

my — incivility last night. This has not been a pleasant vacation for me, but the fault is certainly not yours. I ought not to have —"

"Please! Don't worry about it. Jake told me that tensions were running a little high among you; it's natural that you might not be in a cordial mood. Traveling on a tight schedule can do that."

She sighed. "I'm afraid there's more to it than that. Some of our group . . ." Her eyes slid to Bob, who was still sitting at the very front of the boat, hunched over against the cold and spray, but never moving. "Well, there's been some animosity, but I'll not bore you. I simply wanted to say how sorry I was for my rudeness, and how grateful for your medicine. It's actually rather exhilarating out here on deck, isn't it?"

"Yes, but salt is caking on my face from the spray, and making it a little raw. I wish I had some fresh water to wash it off ."

"Several people are carrying water with them. Perhaps they'd share."

Grace lurched into the cabin with the tipsy gait the boat imposed. I was somewhat surprised when it was Teresa who came to me with a nearly full bottle of mineral water and a clean handkerchief.

"Are you sure you have enough? It seems pretty frivolous, using water to wash my face if you're going to need it to drink."

"I have another bottle, and almost everybody else has at least one. Go ahead. Have a drink, too, if you want."

I took her at her word, and felt much better when I'd mopped the gritty salt off my face and hands, and swallowed a little water to take the taste off my lips.

"That was kind of you, Teresa, thank you." I handed the bottle back to her. "Do you suppose — Bob's up there in the bow getting the brunt of it — maybe he'd like some water, too?"

Teresa's face shut against me; she muttered something and turned to go back into the cabin. I caught her sleeve.

"Teresa, wait!" I said, a little desperately. "I'm sorry if I keep annoying everyone, but I do wish you'd tell me what's going on so I won't put my foot in my mouth every time I open it!"

She looked at me for a long moment, then her face softened and she sat down beside me along the starboard rail. "That's fair," she acknowledged finally. "Our arguments are our own business, but you've been nice to us. You deserve to know enough to keep out of trouble."

I waited while she organized her thoughts.

"It's Bob," she said after a while, keeping her voice low. Well, that came as no surprise after the way she and Grace had acted.

"He's a bit overpious, certainly," I said. "I can see how he might get on people's nerves."

"Yes, but it's a lot more than that. He — he keeps picking at us. You know we're all from different religious backgrounds."

I nodded, with a little grimace.

"I know," said Teresa. "There's a lot of room for hostility there, but we're all civilized. And we all more or less know each other. Even in a city the size of Chicago, there are few enough people who are really active in their churches that we meet now and then. So most of us have a speaking acquaintance. We could deal with our differences if Bob would just leave us alone. But he keeps trying to talk us around to his way of thinking. And he's so obnoxious about it, we get pushed into defending our beliefs more aggressively than we would otherwise. I don't belong to the 'If you're not a Catholic, you're going straight to hell' school of thought — except when Bob's been talking to me. Besides that, he's such a — such a wuss. I don't know how he ever got selected for this trip, unless he's managed to convince people he's as wonderful as he thinks he is."

"I understand he works with young people?"

"Well — he talks a lot about it, anyway."

"And what does Jake think about all this bickering?" I had some idea, but I wanted to hear Teresa's take on it.

"Oh, Jake." She smiled; for a moment she was beautiful. "He's a really nice man, you know? And he can be funny. He tries to laugh us out of it sometimes, but mostly he keeps to himself."

"He's funny? I caught a touch of humor last night, certainly, but I thought he looked basically like a sad sort of man."

Teresa looked at me with something like respect in her eyes, but the smile was gone. "You saw that, did you? He is. It's sort of the 'Laugh, clown, laugh' bit. He's — well, you'd better know this, too, or you might say something wrong again. Jake's life has been pretty tough. He lost his whole family to death, and the last one was a real tragedy. His grandson — he lived with Jake — found out he was HIV positive and killed himself. He was only thirteen."

I drew in my breath.

"Yeah. Don't talk about it, okay? I don't think the others know; I only do because I work with AIDS mothers and their babies, and I hear a lot." She paused. "Makes you wonder sometimes if God really does know what he's doing."

"Teresa," I blurted out, "you are absolutely unlike any other nun I've ever known."

She shrugged. "I'm not a very good one. I got into it mostly because I wanted to *do* something about society, but the rules are pretty frustrating, and the Pope . . ." She rolled her eyes, looking a lot like Jake. "I'm thinking of getting out, if you want to know. Hey, look!"

I had been watching her, not the scenery, but when she pointed I turned and looked, and my mouth dropped open. Nothing I had read, not even the pictures I had seen, had prepared me for this. Staffa is almost impossible to describe, or (as I found out when I had my film developed) to photograph properly.

A small, uninhabited volcanic island, Staffa is made of basalt in the most astounding formations. The top half or so of the island, looking at sheer cliffs rising on the south and east, is made of a higgledy-piggledy mass of curly black rock, exactly like gigantic poodle fur. But about halfway down, there is a line of demarcation so sharp it might have been made by a surveyor. Below it the rock drops to the sea in massive black columns as straight and even as corrugated cardboard. The whole island tilts a bit, as if some giant sea creature were trying to nudge the southern end up out of the water. As we drew closer and could see the mathematical regularity of the columns, perfectly hexagonal in cross section, it became even harder to believe that no human hand had played a part in their shaping. Here were crystals with a vengeance; I could see why the New Agers might be interested.

And then we rounded a point and there was Fingal's Cave, a huge, dark hallway leading into the heart of the island, its walls black columns like organ pipes, its floor the sea, its ceiling more of the columns, their lower reaches evidently broken off eons ago to create this massive formation.

". . . over sixty feet high and two hundred feet deep," came the voice of David MacPherson over the boat's loudspeaker. "Accessible by sea as well as from the island. *Iolaire* willna go through the rocks, but wee boats sometimes go into the cave. If we're able to land, ye can walk to the cave by following the path round to the left from the landing place." The voice ceased.

"What does he mean, *if* we land?" asked Teresa. She had recovered her normal belligerence. "I thought landing was the whole point of this godawful trip."

"Well, the sea's pretty rough, and it looks

70

like there are a lot of rocks," I said dubiously. I would myself be just as happy if the skipper decided not to bring the boat anywhere near the nasty-looking chunks of basalt that came right down to the waterline.

"We'll land," said Jake, coming up beside us quietly. "Look at that harbor." He pointed.

Sure enough, as the boat came around farther to the east and north, the water grew calm. A natural harbor, enhanced by a little pier, made a perfect landing place. Mr. MacPherson brought the *Iolaire* skillfully to a stop, his son tossed out the mooring lines, and we were ready to step ashore. There was one last announcement.

"Ladies and gentlemen, I can give ye no more than an hour on the island. The wind is rising, and I want ye to be comfortable on the trip back to Iona. I'll ask ye, then, to be back on board no later than three-thirty, if ye'll check your watches, please. And if ye hear this signal —" there was a series of four long hoots from the boat's horn "— return at once. *Iolaire* will move offshore, to let others land, but we will return here in aboot forty-five minutes. Enjoy yourselves."

Assisted by young MacPherson, the rest of them clambered up and over the gunwale. At the end of the pier, steep stone steps led up, up, endlessly up to the more-or-less flat surface of the island. I stayed for a little while in the boat, a trifle dismayed now that I had actually seen the terrain. Heights are not my best thing, and arthritic knees make steps, or climbing of any kind, painful and difficult. However, here I was, and here I was unlikely ever to be again. Girding my loins, I followed the rest of the passengers up the steps.

At last, panting, I came to a stop on a little landing where the path divided. I could continue climbing the steps to reach the top of the island, from which there was undoubtedly a splendid view. But if I did that, at the slow pace my knees insisted on, I might not have time to see Fingal's Cave properly, and more important, to hear it. All my life I'd known about the inspiration Mendelssohn had felt when he'd heard the waves booming into Fingal's Cave and reverberating against the back wall. This was possibly my one and only chance ever to hear it for myself, and it was a perfect day for it, too, with high seas making waves that would surely be as impressive as any old Felix had ever encountered.

I turned cautiously to the left and began to edge my way across the natural basalt paving stones that made a narrow, uneven path hugging the cliff.

As I drew closer to my goal, I met some of the passengers coming back. Hattie Mae was clinging tightly to the railing attached to the face of the cliff, and we had to wiggle past each other in a narrow spot. But Grace and Janet sauntered back easily on a lower route, disdaining the railing, and young Chris came along shortly after them, leaping like a gazelle from one rock to another. When Teresa breezed past, she was moving so fast she nearly ran into me at a particularly treacherous spot. I yelped and held on with both hands.

"Oh, sorry," she said, stopping to pant. "I was just letting off some steam." She grinned suddenly. "This island is a great place, huh? I'm having a good time!"

Other passengers I didn't know straggled past as well; I heard one of them say, "We're lucky we got a dry day this time. Last time, with all the mist, these rocks were like glass." I seemed to be the only one still heading toward the cave. I glanced at my watch; I needed to hurry, and the other tourists were right. On the dry rocks, I could safely make a little more speed.

And then suddenly I rounded a rather tricky little corner and there it was. I was at the entrance to the fabled Fingal's Cave, and alone at that, free to gloat without other people's intrusion.

The boom of the water rushing in was all that I could have hoped for. The cave was very dark; a big cloud had moved over the sun. I moved farther into the cave to get the full effect of the sound, and realized there was someone else in there after all, about twenty feet away from me at the very end of the path. Climbing one more basalt step for a better took, I saw that it was Bob. He was looking down, watching the pattern of the waves as they rushed in, eddied, and pulled out again with a strong undertow that oddly left the surface water almost undisturbed; I could see a couple of pieces of wood and a plastic bottle floating in the same place, wave after wave.

Well, Bob was a thorn in everybody's side, but I was a little alarmed for him, all the same. The path was narrow up there and the railing was on the cliff side, with nothing but a few pieces of basalt between the man and the treacherous water below. Not only that, the rocks he was standing on there were shiny and looked wet — and slippery.

"Bob!" I yelled. "Bob, come back!"

I wasn't sure he heard me. The noise of the sea was deafening. I was taking a breath to try again when he looked toward me and I gestured. And then I gasped, as he backed away from me, closer to the edge — and, as I watched in a kind of helpless horror, his feet seemed to slip out from under him and he slithered to the rocky path.

I don't know if it happened in slow motion or if I will simply always see it that way in my nightmares. I do remember moving forward, thinking I could never reach him in time but having to try. He was on his knees. He was on his back, with his hand reaching frantically for the railing that was by now at least a yard away. He was slipping farther, farther over the edge — he was on a narrow rocky ledge far below — he was in the water — he was gone, vanished completely.

I think I screamed. I know I turned to look frantically for help, and saw only a shadow, a flicker, as something — a bird? — moved around the pillars at the entrance to the cave and vanished. "Is anyone there? I need some help! Please!" I looked again, desperately, at the water, and saw only the floating debris, undisturbed even by the body that had fallen through it.

And at that thought I came to my senses and was out of the cave and running for the boat as if all the hounds of hell were after me.

It's a wonder I didn't kill myself on that

wild dash. I took no care for my footing, spurned the handrail, and wobbled more than once as my foot landed on the edge of a rock and slipped off, but I kept on going, waving and shouting as I went.

The *Iolaire* was just coming back in to the landing place; none of the other passengers were in sight. Young MacPherson looked up in astonishment as I skidded down the short pier and stopped, panting.

"We need help!" I managed to say in short jerks. "A man — fallen — in the cave — drowned —"

"Dad! Get the Coastguard!" the young man called before I had even finished. "There's been an accident!" He turned to me. "Come aboard, ma'am, and tell Dad everything so he can report the details."

I was shaking now, so badly that I had to be practically lifted into the boat. A strong young arm supported me and guided me into the cockpit, where Mr. MacPherson took one look at me and pulled a flask from a locker. "Sit doon and drink this," he commanded, his face set, and I obeyed. It was straight Scotch, strong and peaty. I don't especially like Scotch, and I coughed and choked, but after a moment or two my teeth stopped chattering.

Mr. MacPherson had jerked his head toward his son, who took off at a lope toward the cave, and had then turned his attention to the radio. Now he turned to me. "A helicopter and lifeboat will be here within the hour. Can ye tell me what's happened, ma'am?"

I pulled myself together, trying not to shiver. "A man, one of our party, fell into the sea in Fingal's Cave, from the very top of the pathway. He hit a ledge on the way down, and then went into the water. It looked purely accidental — he just slipped and fell. I don't think he can possibly be alive, and anyway he disappeared as soon as he hit the water — the undertow —" I closed my eyes for a moment, and then went on. "I ran back to the boat as fast as I could, but . . ."

"Never mind," said Mr. MacPherson soothingly. "Did ye leave anyone to watch?"

"There wasn't anyone else. I was the only other one in the cave at the time, and I was way down at the entrance. And on the way back I didn't think; I just ran."

My teeth were chattering even worse now, and MacPherson handed me a cup, spooned quite a lot of sugar into it, then poured strong tea from a thermos. It was black with tannin, but the sugar and the heat helped.

"Well, I've sent wee Davie to have a look.

He'll see if there's aught we can do before the rescue team comes."

I giggled just a little at the thought of "wee Davie," who was probably in his early twenties and very nearly as brawny as his father; I wondered how he enjoyed his nickname. Anything to keep from thinking of . . .

"Don't be alarmed, but I'd best get my passengers back." The boat's horn sounded just over my head, making me jump a foot despite the warning. Four long hoots: *return immediately.*

Mr. MacPherson was very kind, and tried to comfort me, but my mind couldn't seem to focus. I kept seeing the cave, with a man about to fall, a man too far away for me to help, too far even to hear me shout over the pounding of the waves, the relentless bass voice of Fingal's Cave . . .

"Dorothy, are you all right? What's happening? No one will tell us."

The other passengers were coming back, and Grace was at my shoulder.

"Dorothy, say something. Captain, this woman isn't well. Someone must take care of her!"

They were swarming into the cockpit, voices raising higher and higher, the Chicago group and the few other passengers. The skipper lost his temper.

"Noo, then!" he roared, and his mariner's voice carried over the nervous crowd and subdued them. "We've an emergency here, and I'll ask ye tae keep your heads, and tae get oot o' my way! Be off wi' ye! Wee Davie has ye all to count. *In the passenger cabin!"* His son, returned from a fruitless search, began herding them out, but the skipper shook his head when I tottered to my feet. "Ye'd best stay. Ye're none too steady on your feet, and I'd as soon you were where I could look after ye."

"They're all accounted for." Wee Davie poked his head in. "Except for — the one."

"Aye. Then ye'd best quiet them, and I'll talk to them." He turned to me. "And what's the puir laddie's name, then?"

"Bob. Bob Williams."

"Ye'll do for a bit?"

"Yes. I'm fine, really."

The boat rocked, creaking a bit at her ropes with each rising swell. I sat and hugged myself and tried not to think of anything in particular while Mr. MacPherson gave the rest of the passengers the bad news.

I don't know if we had to wait a long time for the Coastguard to arrive. I seemed to have lost track of time. I know that Grace came to keep me silent but supportive company, and eventually someone in uniform came to ask me a few questions, and then went away again.

When the skipper came back into the cockpit cabin he looked at me, worried. "I'll radio a doctor to check you over as soon as we make Fionnphort."

"No! No, please don't. I'm all right. I'd just like to get back to solid ground."

Grace, with crisp efficiency, went out on deck, found my purse, and brought it in to me. "Perhaps you need another ginger capsule or two."

I took them gratefully. "Hand 'round the rest to anyone who wants them. I imagine we'll be leaving soon, with the rescue people in charge now."

And indeed, in a few minutes Mr. MacPherson mustered wee Davie to action, and with no wasted words or motions they went into their accustomed departure routine, as if this were the ordinary return leg of a pleasure outing to Staffa. The skipper spoke one last comment into the radio.

"*Iolaire* casting off from Staffa, making for Fionnphort and Iona. Over and oot."

The trip back was no pleasure. Clouds were beginning to mass, so the sunshine was fitful, and the wind and waves were higher, but not alarmingly so. And the ginger capsules worked every bit as well as they had on the way out. But my mind wouldn't let me relax. What could I have done to save Bob? If I had called out earlier, if I had gone farther into the cave . . . I went over it again and again, and there was nothing, and I knew there was nothing, but still I worried.

And when we got back to Iona, what then? What was going to happen? Would the police be involved? This was Scotland, with laws different from England's. And with the missing person an American, everything was going to be very complicated.

At last the boat slackened speed and I saw a pier looming ahead. Wee Davie appeared in the cabin. "Fionnphort," he murmured. "The constable will likely be there to talk to you, ma'am." He went up on deck to help the Mull passengers off the boat, and I waited, apprehensive.

There was, after all, little enough to the interview. The constable from Bunessen asked only a few questions. I assured him that no one had been near Bob when he fell, and that he hadn't jumped, but slipped. He expressed the proper regrets, talked to the other Chicagoans briefly, and then in a minute or two we were headed out again for the trip across Iona Sound. The sea was getting really rough now, and the ten minute trip seemed to last an hour, but eventually we were there, and with wee Davie's help I climbed over the side and jumped down to the pier with rubbery legs. I could have kissed the salty planks, and as a matter of fact I almost did; I certainly couldn't walk. Leaning against a piling, deeply thankful to have my feet on a stationary surface, I tried to recover my equilibrium.

The MacPhersons, as soon as they were free of their charges, began to move the boat out. I watched in horror. "But — but they mustn't go out again in this!" I wailed to no one in particular.

Chris, the last passenger ashore, put a hand on my shoulder to steady me. "There's a good harbor across the Sound, between Mull and a fair-sized island. I heard them talking about it just now. They call it the Bull Hole. The *Iolaire* should be safe there. Whether the skipper and his son can get back across the Sound in a dinghy, or even a launch . . ." He shook his head.

"I hope they don't even try." I shuddered.

"Are you all right?"

"I'm fine." In fact I was just about at the end of my rope. It was time I headed for the hotel, which seemed impossibly far away. I put my head down and trudged, Chris courteously supporting one elbow. I was too far gone even to thank him. At least the wind was at our backs. Drearily I put one foot in front of the other, heading up the hill.

By the time I dragged myself through the heavy front door I had begun to shiver again, and I couldn't seem to stop. Even when I'd settled myself in front of the electric heater that was beaming brightly on the hearth, I shook. The other guests hovered around me, making ineffectual suggestions that I barely heard.

"She's in shock," said Hester Campbell, the proprietor, who came into the room, concerned about the commotion we were creating. "Something's happened?"

Four women began to talk at once.

"Never mind." Mrs. Campbell held up her hand. "Get her up to bed. I'll bring hot water bottles."

It was odd to be talked about as if I weren't there. I tried to say I'd be all right if I could just get warm, but in the end it seemed easier to let someone else deal with the problem. I'd help when I felt more like myself. With no very clear idea of how it happened, I found myself in bed, surrounded with hot water bottles and covered with a thick duvet.

As I began to feel warm, the roar and tumult of the wind receded. I slept.

5

When I woke the room was dark and the wind was howling like a banshee. The old house shook and creaked like the *Iolaire* running on high seas. I sat up and turned on the lamp next to the bed; it was almost eight o'clock. I'd slept past suppertime, but I wasn't hungry; I made no move to get out of bed.

My sleep had not been peaceful. Nightmares were only to be expected, of course. It wasn't, though, the repeated vision of Bob sliding off the rocks of Fingal's Cave that had wakened me, over and over again, bathed in a cold sweat, my heart pounding. It was something much more insidious, something, I realized, that I probably should have told the police.

I kept hearing Maggie McIntyre's voice. *It's a good dry day for Fingal's Cave . . . the rocks are slippery when they're wet . . .*

Where had the water come from?

The rocks had been dry as bone at the entrance to the cave, and all along the outer pathway, as well. The whole path was far above the waterline; even the spray from powerful waves didn't reach that high.

But up at the top of the path, far into the cave where Bob had been, it had looked wet. Why?

I could have been mistaken in what I thought I saw. I've seen enough mirages along roads in the blistering sunshine of an Indiana summer to know that it's easy to see water where none exists. But it had been cold in the cave, with no direct sun, and this hadn't had the shimmery look of a mirage. It had just looked darker than the other rocks, and a bit shiny.

And besides, as I watched once more my mental tape of Bob's fall, I saw what looked exactly like someone trying to keep his balance on a slippery surface.

So again I asked myself: If it was wet, how did it get that way?

That was when I remembered the plastic bottle I'd seen floating in the water far below. Was it a water bottle? Suppose Bob had taken a drink of water out of a bottle like the ones so many people carried in their backpacks. Suppose he had dropped it and it had spilled, the water falling on the rocks and the bottle plunging on down into the sea. Bob sounded like a nitpicky sort of guy, and not overly bright. Would he have leaned forward to see if the bottle was within reach? Tried to catch it as it fell?

Probably. That sounded characteristic.

The trouble was, he hadn't. I had been watching him for a few seconds before he fell. He hadn't dropped anything, leaned over to look for anything. He had just looked at me, stepped backward, lost his footing, and fallen, the best part of sixty feet, crashing against rocks as he went, until he landed in a small, roiling, angry piece of the Atlantic Ocean.

That didn't mean he hadn't spilled the water, of course. He could have, earlier. He wouldn't have known about the hazard of the wet rocks, probably. I hadn't known until a few hours ago, and Bob had been on the island exactly as long as I had. That was almost certainly what had happened. Only an accident.

I tried to punch my pillow into a more comfortable position. The prickling at the back of my neck wouldn't go away.

What if somebody else spilled that water? What if somebody else knew that the rocks would be dangerous when wet? What if there *was* someone behind me in the cave, watching, waiting . . .

The prickles got worse. I had thought I'd seen something disappear around the corner when I'd looked frantically for help. What if it hadn't been my imagination, after all?

The real trouble, I told myself, was that I'd had too many encounters with bodies in the past few months, and most of them had been murdered. There was no question of murder here. I'd been there; I'd seen exactly what had happened.

All the same, I'd have been happier if so many people on the island — in this hotel — hadn't hated Bob.

I was frightening myself, after the manner of children who pretend too much and too vividly, and the knock at the door scared me nearly into fits.

"Mrs. Martin? Are you awake?" Mrs. Campbell's voice came gently through the door.

"Oh! Yes, I — wait a second." I struggled out of the clutches of the duvet and opened the door. "Come in."

"And how are you feeling?" She came in, closed the door, and perched on the edge of the bed. "We've all been *that* worried about you, having to see such a terrible thing."

"I'd never want to see it again," I said with a shudder, "and the worst part was not being able to help at all. I'll probably have nightmares about that for the rest of my life. But I'm fine, really."

She looked at me, brow furrowed. "If you don't mind my saying so, Mrs. Martin, you don't look so well. You're white as that sheet, and you're shaking. You'd best sit down."

I sat on the hard chair that was all the room afforded, more because my legs gave out than at her suggestion. "I wish you'd call me Dorothy. And I do feel a bit wobbly, I admit. I didn't know it until I stood up."

"Well, then, Dorothy, it's my opinion you need food and drink. I came up to see if you'd like a tray in your room. Andrew and I would be happy to —"

"No!" I was still worked up enough to not want to be alone. "No, indeed. I don't want to put you to the trouble. I'm sure you're right, Mrs. Campbell. I just need something to eat. I'll get dressed and come right down."

"It's Hester, please. We did a buffet to-night, in the lounge. Everyone was a bit upset, and it seemed more fitting than a formal meal. There's plenty of food, if you're sure you're able . . ."

I protested once more that I was perfectly all right, and shooed her out. I needed a little more time to think.

Of course my theories and fears were absurd. Bob's death was undoubtedly pure accident. All the same, those prickles weren't going to go away until I could figure out where that water had come from. I'm cursed with a larger bump of curiosity than most people.

I dressed quickly and went down to the lounge. A man I assumed was Hester's husband, Andrew, was tending the buffet, although all the other guests were sitting finishing their meals. All the lamps were lit, and they'd replaced the electric heater with a real fire in the vast fireplace, roaring and crackling and flickering madly as wind blew down the chimney. It added an element of cheer, which was undoubtedly the point. Stan, tail held high, was working the room, exercising his considerable charm in hopes of some tidbits of salmon. The scene, in short, looked cozy, and perfectly normal.

I took a deep breath to relax, took the plate Andrew filled for me at the buffet table, and found a chair near the fire, next to Jake.

Nobody was talking much. I ate a little, and began to feel slightly better. When I had finished, and put my still full plate on the floor for Stan, I turned to Jake.

"I wish people were sorrier Bob is dead," I said quietly. I felt a little shy with him, not certain what to say after Teresa's sad story.

But we were both caught up in the same trouble now, and he was an easy sort of person to talk to.

"Hmm? Sorry, I wasn't listening."

"I keep worrying because nobody's mourning. I know Bob wasn't exactly a pleasant person, but surely we ought to be having a — a kind of wake." I looked around the room. "Only nobody seems to care much."

Jake shrugged fatalistically. "There's no family here, no friends. What do you want, weeping and wailing for a guy we hardly knew, and would have been as happy not to know at all?"

All the same, Jake wasn't eating much, and neither was anybody else. Apart from the tumult of the wind, the room was quiet; the silence thickened. I cleared my throat. "I suppose," I said tentatively to the room in general, "someone ought to let his family know. Or will the Coastguard do that, or the police?"

"Don't know if he had kin," said Hattie Mae. "Never talked about his family — that I heard."

There were nods and mutters of agreement around the room.

"Well, then, his church," I said, trying again. "Someone should call his church.

What time would it be in Chicago? I've forgotten how many time zones away they are."

That at least sparked a brief discussion, since the UK had just switched back from Summer Time to Greenwich Mean Time, whereas America was still on Daylight Savings Time, and no one was sure whether that meant Chicago was now five hours or seven hours earlier than Scotland, rather than the usual six-hour difference.

"Look, why don't I just try to make the call?" I finally said, impatient with them. "It might be easier for me, since I didn't really know him. I don't suppose anyone knows the number?" Of course they wouldn't. Why would anyone carry around the phone number of somebody else's church?

But Grace stood up and went to the bookshelf where she had laid her elegant leather purse. "It's in my church directory. I always carry it, and unless I took it out for the trip — no, here it is. St. Paul's United Methodist Church on Taylor Street." She handed me the book, a small personal phone directory. It listed dozens of churches by denomination, with addresses, phone numbers, and staff names, all in tiny, precise handwriting.

I must have shown my curiosity. "It's for my work," Grace said with a shrug.

"Excuse me?"

"I coordinate soup kitchens all over Chicago," she explained briskly. "I learned long ago that I never know when I may need the help of someone from a neighborhood church, so I compiled this. Please give it back to me as soon as you've finished; it's extremely valuable to me and would take some time to duplicate."

"Yes, of course." Whew! Formidable lady.

"Please use the phone in the office," murmured Andrew, who had been standing by unobtrusively. "Come with me."

Jake followed me, and when I was about to sit down at the desk, he laid a hand on my arm.

"You want maybe I should make the call? I didn't have to see it happen."

I hesitated for only a moment. I felt some responsibility, but it was foolish, I knew. Jake was being a dear. "Thank you so much, Jake. Of course I'd rather you did it. But I'll stay here, in case they want — well, whatever."

"The details they can wait for," said Jake with a frown, and punched in the long series of numbers for an international call.

He was efficient on the phone, very much the important rabbi. "Hello? This is St. Paul's? Speak up, I'm calling from Scotland.

Scotland! This is Rabbi Jacob Goldstein, from Sinai Temple. Is your minister, um — " he consulted Grace's directory "— is Dr. Allen available?"

There was a pause.

"Never mind, then, this is costing money. When he gets back, tell him there's some very bad news. Are you sitting down? I have to break something to you. Yes, it's about Mr. Williams. An accident, yes. I'm afraid it's the worst news — yes. A drowning accident, this afternoon."

Another pause. Jake shook his head impatiently.

"This connection isn't good. I'll fax the details as soon as I can. Look, is there anybody else who should know?" Pause. "Okay, you do that. Yes, we're all very — shocked. Well, I guess he can maybe call if he wants, but it's almost nine o'clock here — no, at night — and we'll be going to bed pretty soon. We're wiped out after all the trouble. Tomorrow would be better. You'll notify the family? I see. Sure. Good-bye."

He turned to me, looking a little gray. "The girl took it hard, wanted to talk about it. I hope her minister knows what he's doing; she's going to need a shoulder to cry on. She said they don't know if he has any family — none in Chicago, anyway. But they'll try to find out." He sighed.

"Well, at least someone is sad about his death. It's almost — obscene — that no one here cares."

Jake shrugged again. "He wasn't an appealing man. The Scriptures talk about casting your bread upon the waters — well, his was soggy and moldy even when it started out."

That was neither a pleasant nor a reassuring thought, however you looked at it. Depressed and apprehensive, I went back to the lounge. It was going to be a long evening.

Andrew appeared at my elbow. "Mrs. Martin, would you perhaps like to finish your wine? We put it away for you; there's a good half bottle left."

I smiled at him gratefully. "That's just what I need. And I'm Dorothy, please. Here, Jake, let's share it and drink it up."

Jake grunted again. "Not me, thanks. Such a headache I had last night! I'll stick to water." He lifted his eyebrows at Andrew, who obligingly brought him a bottle of mineral water and a glass.

So I drank my wine by myself and listened to the wind. It was beginning to fray at my nerves, which were none too steady anyway, and from the electric quality of the silence in the room, I realized I wasn't the only one ready to jump out of my skin. Something had to be done.

And I still wanted to know more about our unpopular preacher.

"I wonder," I said, my voice, raised against the wind, sounding too loud. I lowered it a bit and tried again. "I wonder if anyone can tell me anything about Bob. I know only that he's — he was — a youth minister. Somehow it seems wrong not to — to be able to talk about him."

Teresa spoke first. She sounded oddly angry, but then Teresa nearly always sounded angry.

"He worked at St. Paul's Methodist Church, as Grace told you. It's a very large church, probably about two thousand parishioners. Or whatever Methodists call them. Anyway, it's in a transitional neighborhood. Some of the oldest parts have been gentrified." She spat out the word as if it tasted bad, and Stan, who had fallen asleep in her lap, woke abruptly. She stroked his head, but her tone remained bitter. "Lot of rich people moving in, forcing out the people who lived there. Other parts have gone downhill fast, areas where the gangs are starting to take over. And in the middle there are a bunch of students and young couples with kids in the cheaper houses."

"How you know all that?" asked Hattie Mae, her lower lip jutting out. "Ain't your neighborhood." We could all clearly hear her unspoken postscript, *And you ain't poor or black,* and I held my breath, but Teresa only glared.

"I did a paper on the changing face of Chicago, for graduate school. I wasn't born a nun."

"Yes, well, what is important," put in Grace in her crisp business-executive voice, "is the work Mr. Williams put in to try to make that area a decent place to live in again. He was tireless. He started the youth center on Rush Street, just around the corner from the church, to give the young hoodlums something to do besides dealing drugs on the street corners or killing each other, and he used to spend a lot of his own time there, playing basketball with them, teaching them soccer, that sort of thing. He welcomed everyone, children from all backgrounds and from all over the city. He was a lay worker, you know, not an ordained minister, and I believe he wasn't paid a great deal. And he worked with some of your people, Teresa, to set up the day care center down the street."

"My people? Catholics, you mean? Or Italians?"

Teresa didn't even try to sound polite, and Grace bit her lip. "I meant an order of nuns. I don't know which one. I am not familiar with the more Byzantine structures of the Catholic Church."

"An' what none o'you seem to've figured out," Hattie Mae broke in before Teresa could retort, "is that the kids couldn't stand him."

It was a flat statement, falling like a stone into the room, and the undertext was again clear: *I know about ghetto kids and what they're thinking. You don't.*

Teresa opened her mouth and shut it again.

Hattie Mae went on, her voice just slightly less belligerent. "They went along with it, o' course. Kids are smart, an' they know which side their bread is buttered on. They'd go to 'im with hardluck stories, and he'd fall for it every time, raising money for this and that when the kids were just takin' it to buy drugs. He was too simple to know!"

The silence reverberated.

Grace responded, finally, in her cool, distant way. "Oh, it's true enough that he was a young twerp. Anyone who knew him knew that. But he did do a great deal of work, even if his personality was not — charismatic."

"But what about this award?" I ventured.

"Surely the Religious Assembly — I mean, they must have researched . . ."

Six pairs of eyes looked at me pityingly, including Jake's.

"If," said Chris precisely, speaking for the first time, "the Chicago Religious Assembly were told that Jesus Christ had appeared in person on Michigan Avenue, announcing his candidacy for mayor against Richard Daley, the assembly would take out a full-page ad in the *Tribune* urging everyone to vote for Him. Without making a single phone call."

"I see."

The wind howled, the trees groaned, unknown things out there in the dark crashed and banged, and we sat in depressed silence.

6

One by one we found excuses to go up to bed, but not, at least in my case, to sleep. Oh, I intended to. Feeling that it was a silly thing to do, I nevertheless jammed the back of my chair against the door. With the lever-style handle prevalent in Britain, it was actually a fairly effective deterrent against illicit entry.

So I had taken care of that, and that was absolutely as far as I intended to go in dealing with the absurd idea that I might be housed in the same building as a particularly clever murderer. The evening's conversation hadn't produced anything very productive, and I refused to analyze it further tonight. I was extremely tired, and when I get tired I get cross, and I do not think clearly in that condition. Tomorrow was time enough for pondering. Tonight was for sleep.

It's just possible that I might have managed it, if it hadn't been for the wind. Wind has always frightened me, far more than thunderstorms or blizzards or any of the other weather phenomena I grew up with. I understand it has the same effect on many people. In the parts of the world where a hard wind will sometimes blow for days or weeks, the chinooks in the American West, or the mistrals in France, people go crazy, suicides and murders multiply. Police departments dread the winds.

In my room upstairs, close to the roof of the old house, the wind seemed louder and more threatening than ever. It made me just that much more restless and nervous than I already was, and totally unable to settle myself for sleep. I thought of a hot bath but wasn't sure I wanted to be immersed in water if thunder and lightning should come along to join the party. I said my prayers and recited the Twenty-third Psalm. I counted to a thousand twice, the second time backward, and tried to work complicated multiplication problems in my head. None of the rituals worked.

What I wanted was someone to talk to, someone who would understand, a friend.

My best friend, my husband, was beyond human conversation. That thought didn't bring tears tonight; perhaps part of me had healed at last, or perhaps — well, to be honest, the idea of Alan, alive and sensible and within reach of a telephone, was definitely cheering. I could call him.

I wouldn't, of course. For one thing, much as I wanted to hear his soothing voice, he'd figure out immediately that something was wrong, and it wasn't such a good idea to discuss unfounded suspicions over several hundred miles of international telephone wire. Besides, I wasn't about to call some hotel in Brussels, where it was some unknown hour of the night — probably even later than here — and deal with an operator whose command of English might not be able to cope with an American accent. No, I wouldn't call Alan until tomorrow, but the thought that I could if I wanted to made me feel better.

It didn't allow me to sleep, however. At last I sat up in my rumpled bed and turned on the light. I've never been a smoker, and with the lung cancer statistics what they are, I've always been grateful, but right then I knew what it must feel like to long for a cigarette.

I knew what was wrong, of course. It wasn't really the wind, nor even some stupid fear of a murderer slinking around the hotel. It was my own ambivalence. The sorry fact was that, no matter what might have happened, I didn't want to get involved. I wanted to turn my back on the question of murder, shrug my shoulders, and enjoy my vacation. I'd always despised that attitude in other people, and here I was, searching for an excuse to turn a blind eye to an unpleasant situation.

What situation? part of me whined. *You created the situation yourself, out of your imagination. There's no murder, no reason to poke around, no need to get any further involved with these people.*

I twisted uneasily and punched my pillow, hard. The only trouble with that argument was that I didn't, in my heart of hearts, believe it. With no proof whatever, and only the most tenuous evidence, I thought there was a real possibility Bob Williams had been murdered.

The more fool you!

I was unable to argue with that. The real question, I thought as I climbed out of bed to get a drink of water, was what I was going to do about it.

There were only two options, really. With no police readily available to help, and no friends around I could ask for advice, I could ask questions, trying to keep them innocuous, and always make sure I wasn't alone with anyone. I wasn't likely to find out a thing that was any use, I thought bitterly, and it would mean spending a great deal of time with people whose companionship, for the most part, I wouldn't have chosen.

However, the alternative was to put the matter out of my mind, move to my cottage as soon as possible, and have nothing more to do with anyone involved. And while I could, presumably, carry out the last part of that program, my ill-regulated conscience was not apt to let me forget about Bob, nor about a patch of wet basalt.

I went back to bed resentfully wishing I were less observant, or my glasses less efficient. Eventually I slept.

The wind had gone by morning, though the watery blue sky, with its patchy clouds, left the day's weather very much in doubt. I had slept late and barely made it downstairs in time for breakfast, this time avoiding Stan's recumbent form on the hall floor.

The Chicago crew were all there, reasonably happy together for once, and I was able to get my table for one with no question. The first order of business was a large breakfast. All my life, any trying experience has had the effect of making me first exhausted, then ravenous. Which may help explain why I'm always trying to lose a few pounds. Life is full of trials, and for me they mean extra calories.

Eating alone, I was able to devote myself

to one of the most useful tools of the dedicated snoop — eavesdropping.

"So it's settled," said Grace crisply. "We'll go on the pilgrimage as planned. Now, if we're to be at the Abbey at nine-thirty sharp, we don't have much time. I propose that we assemble there, rather than going over together. Anyone who doesn't make it on time can join us along the way; I understand the route starts off to the south, down to the Nunnery. And don't forget to pick up your sack lunches from the hall table. Right?"

"Yes'm, Miz Gracie, yes'm," muttered Hattie Mae in resentful irony, her lower lip jutting out, and I saw Chris snap off a flippant little salute behind Grace's back, but the rest seemed at least resigned to her assumption of authority. They filed obediently out of the room, and when Jake passed my table he raised his eyebrows and shrugged elaborately. I grinned and put out my hand.

"Wait a minute, Jake. What is this all about? What pilgrimage?"

Another shrug. "So I'm supposed to know? Me, I just do what they tell me."

"Jake, do you ever stop playing the stage Jew?" I asked in some exasperation.

"What do you mean, 'stage Jew'? You

want I should talk like a goy?"

I laughed in spite of myself. "I want you should talk like the educated man you are instead of a caricature of a street vendor. And stop answering every question with another question. I repeat, what pilgrimage?"

He raised eloquent eyebrows, but forebore to shrug, and when he spoke, he had dropped the Yiddish intonations. "I really *don't* know, for sure. Kind of a 'Following in the Footsteps of St. Columba,' I guess. The Abbey people run it every Wednesday, and the big topic this morning was should we go as planned, in spite of Bob, since it's our only chance, and we'd already asked the hotel for sack lunches, blah, blah, blah. Princess Grace finally decided, because everybody else is a fencesitter. All I know is, it's an all-day walk, and if I survive I can go home and tell my cardiologist where to go. Why don't you come?"

"With my knees?" I temporized, thinking furiously about my sleuthful resolutions. "Are you kidding? I'd have to be carried back." Could I find out anything useful if I went?

"I've heard rumors," said Jake, leaning close to my car and hissing in the manner of a late-movie conspirator, "that there are Abbey cars that show up at noon with coffee

105

and tea, and can be commandeered to take the faint-hearted, or weak-kneed, back to civilization." He straightened up and looked at me soberly, for once. "I'd be glad if you came. I could use somebody to talk to."

"Well . . ." Surely there was no danger in such a crowd. And it would be a good opportunity for conversation, with Jake and the others . . .

"I have a compass, so if we fall behind we won't get lost."

"Boy Scouts?"

"YMHA summer camps when I was a kid." He looked at me over the tops of his glasses, his sad spaniel eyes evoking the little boy who proudly found his way out of the woods with his brand new compass. I wondered if he'd taught his grandson woodsmanship, and blinked back a sudden tear.

"Jake, you are a man of parts. Certainly I'll come, but the hotel people won't have a lunch ready for me; I didn't ask for one in time."

Jake scooped up the rest of my breakfast rolls in a napkin and added an apple from the sideboard. "I'll get some butter and cheese from the kitchen, and meet you at the Abbey in —" he glanced at his watch "— five minutes."

I didn't make it in five minutes, of course.

I don't move that fast anymore, and I wasted a few minutes trying to decide whether to call Alan. Probably, I thought, he would be out by now anyway; I'd wait until I got back. I jammed on my hat and managed to catch up with the group as they straggled past the hotel on their way down the hill.

The New Age types were there in force, as well as a number of other people. It looked as though every tourist on Iona was taking advantage of the fleetingly pleasant weather to see the island. The gale had left its mark; bits of trees littered the road, with now and then a slate or two from a roof, but the sunshine held — for now.

"What did I miss?" I demanded as I fell into step beside Jake.

"A prayer, a song. Or hymn, I guess. I didn't know it." His voice had taken on its ironic lilt again, and I looked at him curiously.

"Jake, for a rabbi, you don't seem very interested in religion. Any religion, I mean, not just Christianity. I'd love to know why you became a rabbi." And then I could have kicked myself. He had good reason to question the ways of God to man.

He walked in silence for a few minutes, talk flowing around us, while I tried to think of a way to change the subject.

"I'm sorry, I didn't mean —"

"I was getting my thoughts together. It's a long story, but I'd like to tell you if you really want to know."

"I do."

We had reached the Nunnery by this time, and had to be quiet to listen to the leader's brief history of the place, together with her somewhat indignant speech about the Abbey, devoted to monks, having been restored at great expense, whereas the building devoted to nuns — women — had been left in ruins. She seemed to feel that this bit of history demonstrated once more men's indifference to women's concerns, and it was obvious from Teresa's vigorous nods that she agreed wholeheartedly; myself, I found the ancient serenity of the Nunnery ruins much preferable to the modern bustle of the Abbey, but to each his — or her — own.

There was a Bible reading and another prayer; when we set off again to a ragged chorus of "Marching to Praetoria," Jake told me his story.

" 'Rabbi' means teacher, you know," he began.

"I did know, in fact. I've read all Harry Kemelman's 'Rabbi' books."

"Ah. A most informative series. Then you also know that there is no established body of belief — no dogma, no creed — that one must accept to be a Jew. The Shema — you know the Shema?"

I was pleased that he didn't automatically assume my ignorance. " 'Hear, oh Israel, the Lord thy God, the Lord is One,' " I recited.

He nodded approvingly. "That's about as close as we come to a statement of belief, and it doesn't say a lot — by Christian standards. And of course you know that there are a lot of Jews who don't practice their religion at all. They're still Jews."

I nodded.

"I entered study for the rabbinate because I was in love with learning, not because I was in love with God. I wanted to know, I wanted to be able to argue, I wanted to be a leader for my people. I had a lot of cockamamie ideas back in those days." He shook his head ruefully and was silent for a few minutes while we panted our way up a steep bit of path.

"If you've read Kemelman," he went on when the path leveled out and we had caught up with the rest of the pack, "you will remember that there are no specifically religious duties a rabbi must perform — any adult male can lead prayers. We're not priests."

"Yes, I know all that, but surely — I mean, you do believe in God?"

"I did, once."

The simple phrase fell like a stone.

"Oh, Jake, I'm sorry. I *am* prying into something I have no right to know." I couldn't tell him that I already knew. I stumbled forward, wishing I hadn't been so stupid as to bring it up.

We had reached a rocky area, the footing uncertain and treacherous. Teresa, far ahead of us, close to the guide, bounded over the rocks like a mountain goat. Hattie Mae took one look at what lay ahead, turned on her heel, and headed back, muttering, her lower lip jutting ominously. Jake and I toiled at the rear of the column, my knees beginning to hurt, his face beginning to turn purple.

"Should we stop?" I said anxiously. "We could still find our way back."

Jake didn't waste his breath, just shook his head stubbornly and forged ahead. Well, if he was willing to risk a heart attack, I could stand a painful knee or two. And I had no intention of leaving him alone with his thoughts.

Perhaps fortunately, neither of us had enough breath for talking until our leader took pity on the decrepit members of the group and stopped for a break. Jake and I collapsed onto the nearest big rock, and he took out a bottle of water. Once more I hadn't thought to bring any; Jake offered to share.

"I didn't bring a cup, though." He wiped the mouth of the bottle with his shirt sleeve.

"Niceties be damned." I took a long draft and sat back against a very lumpy rock.

"So do you want to know why?" asked Jake after a little silence.

"If you want to tell me." I didn't have to ask what he was talking about.

"The last straw was my grandson. He was infected with HIV. He killed himself when he found out. He was thirteen."

Even though I knew what was coming, his matter-of-fact tone twisted my heart. "Jake, I — that's —" His voice had been perfectly steady. My own broke, and I could think of nothing at all to say.

Talk flowed around us, the quiet, aimless chatter of people glad to be resting. We sat, marooned in silent thought.

"We'll be moving on now," said our leader after a while, standing and brushing herself off, "up to Loch Staonaig, which is the only source of fresh water for Iona. It seems ironic that an island this small, surrounded by nothing but water, must be very careful about her water supply, but fresh water is a precious gift from God, who provides for all our needs."

She went on for some time in the same vein as the group got to their feet, with bounds or grunts depending on our age, and began to straggle up the hill. I couldn't look at Jake, but he spoke again as we reached the summit.

"You see why it's easier not to believe in God. You believe in a loving, caring God, you're angry all the time, you scream 'Why?' all the time inside, it eats you up. If there's no God it still makes no sense, but you can get on with your life. What's left of it."

"You were very close, you and your grandson?"

"He was all I had left. My wife died when my little Rachel was three — breast cancer. But Rachel was the love of my life, and I got along. She was beautiful, my Rachel — you should have seen her as a bride. I was so excited when she got pregnant, you wouldn't believe. I was like a crazy man."

"What happened to Rachel?" Jake still seemed to need to talk about it.

"You think these things don't happen anymore, but they do. She died in childbirth."

"Your grandson."

"Aaron, yes. His father —" A grimace

passed over Jake's face, and his eyes turned even sadder than usual. "Bernie didn't want anything to do with Aaron. Wouldn't even see him; said the kid had killed Rachel. I was the one who took the boy home from the hospital, and he lived with me until . . ."

"What was he like, Jake? A bookworm or an athlete?"

His face regained a little animation. "Both. Put a book in front of him and he was lost to the world. He read everything — encyclopedias, atlases even — he always wanted to travel, and we had plans —" He stopped, cleared his throat, and went on. "And he was a star athlete. Baseball, soccer, basketball — he was tall for his age, and gangly, but he was strong. He played all over town, not just at his school — I didn't want him to spend all his time with other rich Jewish kids."

"Was he ever involved in any of Bob Williams's teams?"

"No. We live — I live — in the suburbs. He — played against some of Williams's teams." Jake cleared his throat again. He was having trouble with this. "I couldn't keep up with him. He should have been with his father, a younger man who could do things with him, but I couldn't persuade either of them. Bernie softened a little as the years went by, and they saw each other now and then, but Aaron wanted to stay with me, and I'm a selfish old man; I wanted him, too."

"I don't think you were selfish at all. You loved each other — what better environment could a child have? Not that I know a thing about it, really, with none of my own —"

"Count yourself lucky," said Jake flatly. "You don't have them, they can't break your heart."

He moved ahead of me as the trail headed back downhill, and something about the set of his back told me the story was over. I hoped telling it had helped, but I wasn't at all sure.

We struggled on. The sun broke through the clouds and brought heat with it, but my heart wasn't going to warm any time soon.

7

I found going down the hill much harder than going up; Jake silently offered an arm now and then when the going was especially rough, but I was wet with sweat and both knees were almost inoperable by the time we arrived at our next stopping place, the fabled marble quarry. I sank to a grassy bank with a moan and several sharp cracks from tortured joints.

"Careful," said Jake in a politely distant tone that told me he was suffering life-history-teller's remorse. "Behind you."

I swiveled my head and saw the sharp, rusty spikes of some unidentifiable piece of ruined machinery a few inches from my back. "I'll just have to take my chances," I said firmly. "I am not moving from this spot until I cool off and my knees stop screaming at me."

"You must focus on your inner being," said a serene individual seated cross-legged on the grass a few feet away. "If you're really centered, you won't feel any pain."

I looked at him — her? — with interest.

The person, of whichever sex, had long dishwater-blond hair pulled back in a ponytail, a sensitive face with pale blue eyes, and beautiful, expressive hands. The sweatshirt read BE TRUE TO YOUR KARMA, and its dark blue showed off the pyramid shaped crystal dangling below the neck.

"And just how do I do that?" I asked. "Focus on my inner being, I mean."

"Look inward. Meditate. Concentrate on the oneness of the universe."

It sounded a trifle vague. I obediently tried looking inward, but my meditations seemed to focus on my stomach, which growled.

"I guess I'm not good at this. I must admit my knees don't hurt as much." True. Rest was doing them some good. "Where are you from?" Better change the subject before I revealed the true depths of my ignorance.

"I'm from Los Angeles. Well, close to Los Angeles. Most of us are from Southern California."

Of course. "Really. I have a niece in Chatsworth, and a sister who lives in Ventura County." And both of them reasonably normal people. Not everyone who lives in Southern California is crazy. "You must be part of the group at the Argyll Hotel. How many of you are there?"

"Thirteen. That's a lucky number, really, you know. We set it up that way on purpose."

"And why did you come to Iona?"

She — I had tentatively decided the person was female — replied earnestly. "Partly the basalt crystals on Staffa. They're very powerful. But we're interested in all religions; there is truth to be found everywhere if you open yourself up to it. Iona is a home for the old religions, too, you know. The Druids had shrines here long before the Christians came. And Wicca — here, in this place, can't you feel it?"

Well, yes, I could. The sun had disappeared again, but the chill I felt wasn't entirely physical. Deirdre the wagon driver had been right. There was evil here in the marble quarry.

Of course, according to my own old-fashioned beliefs, the possibility of evil exists wherever there are human beings, with their fatal propensity for messing up whatever they touch.

I looked my solemn adviser squarely in the eye. "How old are you, child?"

She drew herself up and frowned. "Nineteen."

"Then let me tell you something you may not have had time to learn for yourself. Yes, truth can be found in many places, but there are different kinds of truth, and some kinds can be deadly. Before you 'open yourself up' to just any influence, you'd better be sure you know which kind it is."

It was a pompous enough little speech, if well meant, and of course it was futile. She knew everything; people that age do. I could see in her suddenly glazed eyes the thoughts she was too polite to utter: old fogey, close-minded, stuffy. I sighed and breathed a quick prayer that the benign influences of Iona might wash some of the nonsense out of her head.

Our leader was standing up again. "We'll go from here over to Columba's Bay, where he and his monks first landed at the end of their voyage from Ireland. After we spend a little time there, we'll make our way back to the Machair for lunch."

There were glad sounds greeting the word "lunch." I tried to smile at my New Age friend, but she had turned her back and made herself very busy gathering up her gear. Jake had disappeared, as well. But Teresa was nearby, so I asked her. "What's the Machair? And how far is it?"

"It's that grassy meadow we passed on the way here. You know, where the golf course is?" Teresa was the kind of person who always knows things, but I didn't appreciate her information.

"But that's *hours* away!" I wailed.

She grinned. "We came very slowly, and stopped a lot. It'll be quicker going back. It's only a little over a mile, actually."

"And all vertical, I'm willing to bet," I said darkly.

"Almost all," she agreed cheerfully, and then lowered her voice. "Mrs. Martin — Dorothy — I overheard what you said to that little idiot." She cocked her head toward my long-haired companion, now fortunately out of earshot.

"I suppose you thought I was a preachy bore," I said, embarrassed.

"Not at all. Those New Age people actually believe in suppressing their critical faculties, so they sometimes swallow the most pernicious nonsense. You were absolutely right, and I'm glad you said it. Um — do you need any help? Because otherwise —"

I shook my head, she strode off, and I shook my head again to try to clear it. I'd have thought Teresa, ultramodern nun that she was, would sympathize with the truth-is-everywhere clan. Instead she'd agreed with my conservative views, and quite amiably — for her.

Could her good mood possibly have anything to do with the fact that Bob Williams was dead?

I wasn't learning anything very useful, was I? And I didn't enjoy being suspicious of everyone I talked to, but what choice did I have? I kept up the smartest pace I could on the way back over the hill. I wasn't eager to be left alone.

The smartest pace I could manage, however, was, in fact, pretty slow. Ordinarily I'd have been sure there was no way at all that I could get over the marshy, rocky hills to Columba's Bay, but I did it somehow. From there to the Machair was even worse, but I managed that, too. I was trembling with fatigue when I finally found a little hillock where I could sit, too tired to be hungry anymore, but possessed of a raging thirst.

It was Grace who came to my rescue with a plastic cup of water from the Abbey van's supply. She also fetched my rudimentary lunch from Jake, and insisted I eat it. All her ministrations were conducted with an air of impersonal detachment, as though her mission in life were to took after the hungry, and she intended to do it — whoever they were and wherever she found them.

When I had recovered a little I tried to talk to her. "Tell me about your work with the soup kitchens, Grace," I began. "It sounds interesting."

"Does it?" she replied coolly. "I doubt you would find it so."

"Well, but — you must run into fascinating people."

"Not really." She picked up a sandwich and looked away, presenting to me the back of her perfectly groomed head.

I was left with the feeling that I had been trying to crack a Fabergé egg. It was exquisite to look at, but smooth and cold to the touch, and utterly impenetrable.

I went back to the hotel with the Abbey people. Too much exercise and too much heart-wrenching had drained both soul and body; I was in no shape either to climb Dun I, Iona's highest hill, or to appreciate the view once I got there. So I hobbled straight up to my bed, propped the chair under the door handle, and fell into the dreamless sleep of physical exhaustion. I woke a couple of hours later, stiff but rested, and ravenous.

The hotel was quiet. I looked both ways before stepping out of my room, but no one was around, nor was anyone in the lounge — except Stan, abandoned to sleep on a couch in the total relaxation only a cat seems able to achieve. Hattie Mae was evidently out or napping. Dinner was not yet in preparation, so the kitchen was cold and silent.

There was no one to beg for a snack. Although exercise wasn't high on my list of priorities right then, calories were. And my neck was getting stiff from looking over my shoulder.

I moved my aching body out the door and down the hill to the village shops.

Fifteen minutes later, somewhat fortified by some melt-in-the-mouth candy called "tablet" — sort of a vanilla fudge — I wandered toward the other end of the village.

There was no traffic in the Sound today. The crashing waves provided the explanation; in the mysterious depths of the sea the storm had not yet worn itself out, and this was no place for small boats.

I didn't linger at the jetty, but walked down the street, and as I passed the minute post office, decided to turn in. Hope springs eternal.

Surprisingly enough, in this case it was justified. I hadn't yet opened my mouth to make my inquiry when the postmaster handed me an envelope.

"Ah, ye'll be Mrs. Martin, I've nae doot. I've a letter for ye. The post was late today, due to the gale and it havin' to be brought by special ferry, but it's come noo, and if I'm no' mistaken, ye'll be findin' the key to yon cottage in it. I was juist goin' to take it up to ye."

He handed over a slim packet with, sure enough, a bump in it. I tore it open.

"Dorothy, hope this is the right key. Found it under umbrella stand; suspect Samantha." (Samantha was my young Siamese, who would chase anything she could get her busy little paws on. I was lucky she'd pushed her trophy under the umbrella stand. It could just as easily have been shot into the wilderness under the refrigerator and lost forever.)

"Gorgeous weather here, last of the summer. Your asters thriving. Hope having good time. Jane."

I chuckled. Jane's note was so like her. Brief, businesslike, no nonsense about "Dear" or "Love." But she'd taken considerable trouble to search my house for the key. I'd have to find her a really nice thank-you gift, which she would accept with gruff disclaimers, but would secretly treasure.

"*Thank* you, so much!" I beamed at the postmaster. "You were right; it is the key." I didn't ask how he knew about the key. I'd lived in Sherebury long enough to know that small towns in this part of the world know everything about everybody. Here in a tiny community like Iona, a person probably couldn't snarl at her husband in bed one night without getting anxious queries about her marriage the next day. I was a little more curious about how he knew who I was, out of all the Americans on the island, but I didn't like to ask.

"Good! It's a fine wee cottage; ye'll enjoy it. And may I say that's a bonnie wee bonnet ye've got on?"

I'd forgotten my tam-o'-shanter, which I'd jammed on as I'd left the hotel. Well, my hats do tend to make me recognizable. I smiled my appreciation of his compliment as I made my way out the door and up the short path to the village street.

At the head of the path, I hesitated. Left or right? The sensible thing would be to go back to the hotel and collect my luggage, but I was eager to see my new domain. I turned right.

I moved along at the leisurely pace my aching muscles preferred, looking over the gardens on the seaward side of the road. On the whole, they hadn't fared too badly in the gale. Some of the flowers had been blown off the fuchsia hedges, and the more fragile annuals and perennials lay prostrate and discouraged, but the gardens were sheltered by walls and hedges, and Iona gardeners were doubtless used to severe weather, and planted accordingly.

The houses, on the other side of the street, were the same. Here and there a slate was missing, a chimney pot askew. But the day was wearing on, and most of the damage, I imagined, had already been repaired by the hard-working householders. The houses were small and sturdily built, meant, like the gardens, to withstand the severities of life on an isolated, windswept island.

My house (I had already begun to think of it as mine) was charming. Outside it was as plain and solid as the rest, a gray stucco box with blue shutters and a little blue roof forming a tiny porch for the front door. But there was a window box under both lower front windows, planted with bright pink geraniums that seemed to have weathered the storm unperturbed, and the snowy curtains visible in the front windows promised a well-kept interior. I let myself in with anticipation.

The layout of the house was very simple. A minuscule front hall had doors leading to a small living room on one side and an even smaller dining room on the other, with the kitchen at the back. Steep, narrow stairs led to two bedrooms and a small bathroom. It was nothing more than your basic two up and two down, in fact, but made delightful by the way it was furnished — simply, even sparsely, in white, mostly, with a few bright cushions and pretty watercolors.

Someone with excellent taste had managed, in fact, to give a tiny house the feel of spaciousness and repose. No wonder Lynn loved it here. It was, to be sure, in stark contrast to her London house, which had Renoirs and Sargents on the walls, and wildly expensive (and lovely) antique furniture. It didn't resemble my house much, either, although most of what clutters mine is just that — clutter. But contrast is part of what a vacation is all about. I was going to love it here.

I inventoried the kitchen carefully before I left. A former tenant had kindly left behind some coffee and a tin half full of tea cookies, and the basics of housekeeping — flour, sugar, salt, a few spices — came with the cottage, but I would certainly need to lay in supplies before I could actually live here. I started a list on the pad thoughtfully placed by the telephone. Bread, orange juice, eggs — no, I had to remember Tom's heart problems, no eggs — cereal, that was it. I went on through canned soup and sandwich material for lunches, and some salmon and vegetables, stewing beef and salad stuff for a couple of dinners. That would do it until the Andersons arrived, anyway. Tucking the list in my purse, I headed joyfully out the door.

And does this mean, my nasty inner voice piped up, *that you intend to forget about Bob?*

I sighed. Try as I might, I *couldn't* forget about Bob. But surely I could be allowed to defer the problem for a little while?

As I was nearing the Argyll Hotel, a door opened in the cottage just beyond and David MacPherson popped out, making me hope I hadn't been muttering to myself.

"Mrs. Martin! Have ye a moment?"

"Of course, Mr. MacPherson." I was glad to see him, actually; he just might have some news that would mean I could stop worrying. Exactly what news that might be, I didn't stop to define.

"Would ye like to step inside for a cup of tea? My wife's juist set it to brew."

"That sounds very nice, thank you." Actually, if the tea was anything like what had been in his thermos yesterday, I'd have to be very cautious and add a lot of milk, but as my father used to say with a twinkle in his eye, "Never suppress a generous impulse."

I was introduced to Fiona, his attractive wife, and, of course, I'd already met young David. The family was just sitting down to

127

their tea, and I made only a token protest when I was offered fresh scones and short-bread. The tea was, indeed, too strong for my taste, but lots of milk and sugar made it drinkable, and the food was heavenly. I slathered butter on a hot scone, lumpy with currants, and told myself firmly that I deserved it. Anyway, I'd worked it off this morning. Of course I indulged in these rationalizations far too often, but *this* time it was justified. Sure it was. I defiantly accepted another piece of shortbread.

While we ate, the three MacPhersons kept up a gentle flow of conversation about the gale and the other villagers, whose roof had been damaged, whose garden needed work. The two men, father and son, had made it home easily in the dinghy after mooring *Iolaire* in the Bull Hole for the night. They plainly thought me too easily impressed by a wee blow, while I was filled with awe at the thought of anyone crossing the Sound in a small boat in that weather.

"Was the *Iolaire* damaged at all in the storm?"

"Nay. She'll ride oot a wee gale like yon. She's a good boat, Mrs. Martin, and we take good care of our boats here on Iona. For islanders, they're a lifeline. But we'll no' be able to take her oot soon; there's too big a swell for passengers."

"Then I suppose the Coastguard hasn't been able to — find anything. Or do you know?"

"Aye, I've a radio in the house as well as on the boat. They've been oot since first light, in boats and helicopters, and the police have been sairchin' the shore, as well. They've no' found anything yet."

"Will — do you think the body will stay in the cave, or be washed out to sea?" I thought about the impression I'd had of a strong undertow.

He thought about that for a moment, and then shook his head. "I dinna know. Debris that floats, wood and that, can stay for weeks in the cave, but something heavy . . ." He shook his head again. "We'll have to let the Coastguard sort it. It's their job."

I thought about Bob's body, being dashed against the rocks, finally floating, but perhaps unrecognizable by then . . . I decided not to think about it.

"Ye know the police will be on the island soon, to question you and the others."

I put my teacup down carefully, hoping the jerk of my hand hadn't spilled tea on the carpet.

"Oh," I said as soon as I thought I could control my voice, "the police? Why is that?

We already talked to the constable once."

"Sudden death," he said laconically. "Or presumed death, but the Coastguard willna find him alive, if they find him at all. The currents round here can be verra unreliable, and a gale like yon . . ." He shook his head. "Wi' the sea running as it is, the constables'll no' be here soon, I'm thinking. They're no' worried about foul play, and they'll no' want to get oot in a dinghy; they'll wait for the ferry."

"I wondered about that." Change the subject.

"I haven't seen the ferry today. Do they take it to some safe harbor in a storm?"

"She's in the Bull Hole wi' the rest, and she'll stay there for a bit. She can handle a bit of weather, but her computers can be touchy, and Cal-Mac willna take chances when it's too rough."

"Cal-Mac?"

"Caledonian MacBrayne," explained Fiona softly. "They offer the ferry services for the whole of the Hebrides."

"Do ye not know the auld rhyme?" David asked me.

"What old rhyme?"

" 'The airth belongeth to the Lord, And all that it contains, Excepting for the Western Isles, And they belong to MacBrayne's!'

Caledonian MacBrayne has run the service for the islands for generations, time oot o' mind."

There was something comforting about the thought of a continuity like that, "time out of mind." Maybe part of the eternal peace of Iona had to do with that sort of changelessness.

But there was no peace for me until I settled a few things, at least in my own mind. I rose. "Thank you, Mrs. MacPherson, for a lovely tea. I must get to the hotel to check out." I thought about adding that I was now staying in Dove Cottage, but everyone on the island who cared probably already knew that my key had arrived.

"There's a shortcut, if ye're in a hurry," said Mr. MacPherson, plainly considering a hurry to be an odd, foreign sort of idea. No one except tourists hurried on Iona, but he was ready to oblige if I really wanted to do so. "Juist the other side of the Argyll, a footpath. There's a fuchsia hedge for a good part of the way; mind the bees."

"Thanks, I will. When — um — when do you think the police might get here, Mr. MacPherson?"

He shook his head and looked at me with those direct blue eyes, rimmed with a sailor's wrinkles. "My name's Davie. We'll know each other well enough before this is over, I've nae doot. I dinna know when the constables may be on Iona. Ye see, a storm's on its way, a real one, they say. Coming tomorrow, next day. I hate to tell ye, but this island may be cut off for two, three days."

8

I decided to make my hotel stop first, and then stock up on groceries. For one thing, though the Campbells weren't the sort to hold me to a rigid checkout time, they deserved as much notice as possible that I wouldn't be in to dinner. I supposed I should also pass the word about the storm, and perhaps, though I was reluctant, about the probable visit from the constabulary. I *was* in a hurry, so I found the footpath and followed its winding way, fighting the unwise impulse to shoo away every bee that happened across the path.

By the time I got back to the Iona, the rest of the group had returned from their afternoon's exertions. They were sitting around in various poses of exhaustion, waiting for tea to be served. I was in no danger of being cornered alone by one of them.

Only Hattie Mae showed any signs of animation. "Come over here and talk to me, honey." She patted the seat of the couch next to her. "All the rest of 'em is too tired to do nothin' but moan."

"I can well believe everyone's tired," I said, sitting down with some reluctance. The Campbells were apparently busy elsewhere, though, so I supposed I might as well talk to her. Kill one more bird. "Just the morning half of the walk wore me out. I'm glad I went, though — in retrospect."

"I guess that means you wouldn't want to do it again, huh?" Hattie Mae laughed, a deep, warm laugh that startled me. It was the first time I'd encountered her acting genuinely pleasant. She and Teresa both in one day . . .

I laughed in return, and hoped it didn't sound hollow. "Well — not for a while, anyway. I wish I were in better shape, though. It's disgraceful how I pant and toil away, when someone like Teresa just bounds along."

"Honey, you and me ain't never again gonna be as young as her, nor as skinny, neither. Nor as downright blind-as-a-bat stupid."

What did that mean? "Teresa's actually quite well educated, you know," I began, but Hattie Mae shook her head with heavy patience.

"I ain't talkin' book-learnin', honey, I'm talking deep-down ignorance. Sociology, huh! Social means people, and what she don't know about people'd fill all the books in her college liberry. She's got all these high-flown ideas, but she just ain't lived long enough, or hard enough, to know nothin'. 'With the ancient is wisdom; and in length of days understanding.' Job 12:12."

I wasn't sure whether Hattie Mae was calling me ancient, or herself.

"I guess she means well," she added grudgingly. "We had us a little talk this mornin' about that Bob, and she was all for not speakin' ill of the dead and that. Even quoted the Bible at me; First Corinthians 13."

She gave me a quizzical look, and I nodded my familiarity with St. Paul's essay on Christian love. She must think me a real heathen if she thought I wouldn't know that! I wondered how she would react if I told her it had once helped me discover a murderer, but she swept on.

"I told her charity was all very well, but I believe in tellin' the truth and shamin' the devil, and the truth is, that boy was no blessed use to nobody, includin' himself. I was willin' to go along with him when he was alive, bein' charitable like Teresa says, but I don't see no call to make a saint of him now he's dead.

"You, now, you seem kinda sensible, and

you ain't afraid to tell a person off, like you did me yesterday morning."

I looked at my lap and fidgeted.

"No, I ain't sayin' you was wrong. This here tragedy we done had in our midst showed me I was bein' too harsh. 'Judge not, that ye be not judged.' Matthew 7: 1."

"The Sermon on the Mount," I murmured, and Hattie jumped on it.

"So you do know your Bible!"

"No, no," I said with the embarrassment of an Episcopalian accused of a specific Christian virtue. "Bits and pieces, is all. But Hattie Mae, I still don't quite understand what you had against Bob. I mean, nobody liked him, but everyone else seems to feel he was doing a good job, and making some personal sacrifices for it, too. Why are you so sure you're right?"

This was risky. She looked at me hard, her brown eyes turning flat and dark and challenging, and finally answered my question with a question of her own. "You got kids?"

"No." I didn't feel like elaborating on how much Frank and I had wanted them, how hard it had been to accept, finally, that they weren't going to happen.

"If you got kids you care about, and you live in a place like Chicago, you gotta keep your eyes open about the people they go with, and you get a feelin'. A good feelin' or a bad feelin'. I had a bad feelin' about Bob Williams. Never nothin' I could put my finger on, so I didn't say nothin', not while he was alive. But I *know* the kids laughed at him behind his back, 'cause I heard mine doin' it. They didn't have no respect for him, for sure, and there's things they coulda told me, only they wouldn't. You know how kids are. Well, maybe you don't, seein' as how you never had none, but —"

"I taught school for nearly forty years," I interrupted. "I know what you mean. Yours are teenagers, then?" That's the age when they clam up, usually. I had preferred fourth-graders, who were still open and friendly, although the last few years I'd taught, they were starting to act older and more obnoxious. Kids grow up too soon these days.

"Harold, Jr., he's fifteen, and Michael's twelve." She fumbled in her purse and drew out a folder full of pictures. "Harold's on the baseball team; he's a little squirt like his father and can't play no basketball or football. Michael, he thinks he's named after Michael Jordan, which he ain't, and he thinks he's gonna *be* Michael Jordan, which he might — he's pretty good."

"They're good-looking boys. You must

be proud of them."

"They're good kids. Go to a good Christian school, the same one my mama sent me to. And we live in a decent neighborhood, but you never know these days. We can't afford to buy 'em all the stuff they want, fancy shoes and jackets and I don't know what all, and I get scared they'll start dealin' drugs to get what they want. I've tried to bring 'em up right, but . . ." She sighed deeply, and I shook my head in sympathy.

"It isn't easy being a parent now. I don't suppose it ever was. But look at you. I don't suppose your parents had all the money in the world, either, but you turned out all right. Did you go to music school?" I still wanted to know more about her.

"No, my mama said I'd better learn somethin' I could make money at, so I studied to be a secretary. She scrubbed floors nights so's I could go, and I didn't care much for it, but I went. That's how I got the job at the church, and that's how I got to be the choir director, in the back door, you might say; filled in when the old director got sick." Hattie fell into a reminiscent tone of voice. "I was just the church secretary then, but I'd always been good at music — piano, singing. My mama wouldn't let me get into the commercial end of it, neither, said it was no life for a girl, always on the road and mixin' with riffraff. She was real strict, my mama. Still is, for that matter. She's stayin' with the boys these two weeks. Big as they are, you can't take no chances with kids, the way the world is these days, and their daddy's gone a lot; he drives a truck."

"What is your church?"

She lifted her head in a proud gesture. "You ever hear of First African Baptist?"

"Good heavens, yes, I've seen them on television. They have the most wonderful music — you don't mean to say you . . . ?"

She nodded complacently, her chins compressing.

She deserved the self-congratulation. Chicago's First African Baptist Church is famous, at least throughout the Midwest. The sort of rock gospel music they perform is utterly foreign to my own more austere church music tradition (Palestrina, Byrd, Thomas Tallis, Ralph Vaughan Williams), but in its own way it's absolutely first class. When I lived in Indiana I used to watch the televised services occasionally. Frank never understood why I liked them, but there was something about their enthusiasm that stirred my soul, and the musicianship was thoroughly professional. It was like really

139

good jazz: improvisatory, intensely personal, and for me genuinely exciting. I looked at Hattie Mae with new respect.

"I had no idea. Have you been doing this long?"

"Fifteen years."

Then it was her choir I'd watched.

"I'll bet you make a lot more money now than you did as a secretary."

"I do all right. Mama still keeps at me about it, though. Says it ain't steady, and I better keep practicin' my typin'." She chuckled. "I tell 'er ain't nobody uses a typewriter no more, and I don't know nothin' about them computers, so I'll just have to stick with what I'm doin'. Makes her mad, I hope to tell you!"

Hester came in just then with tea, and I jumped up. "Hattie Mae, I must go. I'm moving into my cottage. I want to hear you sing, sometime before you leave Iona!"

I intercepted Hester before she could leave the room. "Hester, I'm so sorry, but the key to my cottage arrived, and I'll be leaving the hotel. I wish I'd known sooner, so I could give you some notice."

"Don't worry. The only thing is, I'll have to charge you for dinner tonight, since we've begun cooking it. So you may as well stay and eat it, as you're paying for it!"

I laughed with her. "I won't stay, but I'll come back. I want to get to the store before it closes. But if you can make out a bill for me, I'll settle up later, and get my belongings out of your way. And, Hester —" I drew her aside and lowered my voice "— I've been talking to David MacPherson. He says another storm's coming, a bad one, in a day or two. And either before it gets here or after it passes, the police are going to want to talk to everyone again about the — er — accident."

Hester sighed. "Aye, we've heard the weather forecast. It's not good. And the police —" She shook her head. "That creates a problem. Our duty is to our guests, and they're planning to leave Friday. Mrs. Desmond told me their flight back to America leaves from Prestwick Saturday morning. So we daren't delay them, but if the police don't hurry . . ."

I saw what she meant. Prestwick is the airport that serves Glasgow. If the Chicago group were traveling by train they'd need to leave by the first ferry Fridav morning in order to make the connections to get them back to Glasgow on time. It was now (I checked my watch) quarter to five, and this was Wednesday. Even if the waves calmed suddenly, the ferry wouldn't operate today.

141

If the storm came early tomorrow, my compatriots could kiss their plane good-bye. On the other hand, if good weather stuck around for a while, and for some reason the police didn't make it, the Campbells were going to be in the position of requesting that their guests stay, when staying put their travel plans in jeopardy.

"Indeed," I said thoughtfully. "Well, I must get to the grocery store. Let's hope for the best, both from the weather and from the police. I'll be back soon."

"Would you like to borrow my trolley? I use it when I've a few supplies to get and Andrew has the car."

I gratefully accepted the loan of her folding, wheeled shopping cart, and sped down the hill.

It took the best part of an hour to buy the items on my list (to which I added rolled oats to please the clerk, who was horrified at the idea of breakfast without porridge), cart them to the cottage and put the perishables away in the minute refrigerator, and speed back to the hotel by the footpath, Hester's cart bumping along behind me.

There was no one in the hall but Stan, who smelled the salmon I had been carrying. He gave the cart a thorough, hopeful examination before looking at me and meowing his deep disappointment that nothing edible was left.

"You, my lad, are quite fat enough, you know," I informed him. "However, if you come and see me tomorrow, I might have a snack for you anyway!"

He made no promises, but I reflected, as I went upstairs to pack, that I wouldn't be at all surprised to see him turn up. Stan rather liked me, and he was a shameless beggar.

I am continually amazed by how much clutter I can create in a room, even when I occupy it for only a few days. I was just re-checking all the drawers, and my favorite place for forgetting things, the back of the bathroom door (I've lost more bathrobes that way), when a knock on the door announced Andrew, ready to take my bags down.

"I'll run you down in the car," he said amiably, picking up most of the pile of assorted bags, cases, and boxes. "You'll not be able to manage that lot by yourself."

"You're right about that, and I do appreciate the offer. You and your wife have certainly been nice to me; in a way I'll miss the Iona."

Then I was afraid he would misinterpret my careless remark, but he simply grinned and started down the hall.

As we drove to the cottage, the ineffable peace of Iona seemed a tangible thing. The clouds were beginning to gather, and they deepened the twilight, but there seemed no threat in them. Maybe the forecasters were wrong; maybe there would be no serious storm. The velvety quiet, the yellow lights shining from cottage windows, the silhouette of the Nunnery, timeless and serene against the fading light — I heaved a deep sigh. Why did people and their problems have to intrude on such perfect beauty?

Andrew offered to drive me back up to the hotel, but I shooed him away. I wanted to unpack and get settled, and it was less than a ten-minute walk. I needed all the walking I could get in, anyway, to offset the stiffness brought on by the morning's unaccustomed exercise, not to mention the shortbread and tablet and scones and all the other goodies I'd been eating nonstop ever since I'd landed on Iona.

Ever since I'd landed. Good heavens, could it have been only two days ago? I felt I had lived through a hundred years since Monday. Soon, now, I'd be safely alone, and could sort out everything that had happened, and what little I had learned about the Chicagoans.

They weren't actually as bad as I'd

thought at first. Grace might have an unbreakable shell, and I'd had no chance to talk to Chris or Janet, but certainly Jake was a pleasant man, and he had borne the tragedies in his life with great courage. Hattie Mae had her redeeming qualities, and even Teresa had been quite civil this morning.

I'd think about why later.

I puttered and fussed, taking longer than I should to unpack, put away the rest of the food, and settle myself in my domain. By the very last of the light I picked a few flowers from the back garden, those that hadn't been flattened by the gale, and crammed them into a water glass. I was going to be late for dinner at the hotel if I didn't hurry.

I had to find my flashlight. Iona has little outdoor lighting, and if there was such a thing as a moon, it was hidden by clouds that evening. I'd have to take the shortcut to make it on time, and those high hedges would cut off what little light there might be. Fortunately, I hadn't had time yet to lose the blasted flashlight; I found it (amazingly) exactly where I had put it half an hour before, and set out.

The path had more twists and turns than I had remembered. Things always look different in the dark, and more than once I was convinced I was lost. It was impossible, of course; the path only led up to the road above, with no choices to make, no wrong turns to take. But with the only light the rather feeble cone cast by my small flashlight, I might as well have been in a maze. Twigs reached out and touched my sleeves; small insects blundered against my face. The hedges closed in and my claustrophobia gathered itself to pounce. I was nearly running, and panting like a warm dog, by the time the path opened out and I arrived in a little field, with only one gate between me and the road. Then scudding clouds receded for a moment, the moon shone benignly, and Iona was its peaceful self once more.

I wished I could embrace that peace.

9

I'd had little chance all day to call Alan, and now it would have to wait until after dinner. I was late as it was, and it would not only be much easier to make the call from the phone in the cottage, it would also be more private, in case — well, just in case.

When I got into the dining room, I saw that the groupings had changed. Jake was sitting at a small table with Chris, Teresa with Hattie Mae — the mind boggled — and Janet and Grace at a table for four. I could either join them and try to learn something, or eat alone.

"Do you mind?"

Janet looked as though she did, very much, but Grace lived up to her name and gestured to one of the empty chairs. "Please."

As it turned out, I didn't talk much to anyone, for the Campbells chose that night to serve haggis. I'd eaten it before, when some Scottish friends of Alan's had invited us to dinner, and I didn't mind it. It's a concoction of ground meat (beef or mutton or other things; I'm told it's best not to ask), onions, spices, and Scotland's ubiquitous oats. The classic method of preparation is to stuff the mixture into a sheep's stomach (duly cleaned, one assumes) and steam it. It comes out like a sort of hash, with the oats substituting for potatoes. It's *the* traditional dish for Hogmanay (New Year's Eve), and is served up with great ceremony, they say, brought in stomach and all, and slit open with a sword if one happens to be handy.

The staff had dished it up in the kitchen, so there was no stomach in evidence, but conversation in the room still came to a halt as the food was served. The aroma was savory, though the gray mess looked rather unappealing.

Grace poked fastidiously with her fork. "What is it?" she asked in her most patrician voice.

I explained, judiciously omitting some of the more colorful details. "It's Scotland's national dish, very special. We're being honored."

"I see." She picked up a minute forkful and tasted it, and then without a word began to eat, applying herself diligently and drinking a lot of water.

Janet sat and glared alternately at her plate and at Grace.

"How can you eat that — garbage?" she finally said. I was quite sure another noun had been her first choice.

"It's a sin to waste food," Grace replied briefly, and went on with her meal.

"It's actually pretty good, no matter how it looks," I said placatingly. "Although mutton is something of an acquired taste, I suppose. You get a lot of it on this side of the Atlantic."

"*You* may. I don't." Janet shoved back her chair, picked up her plate, and marched to the kitchen door. The young waiter was just coming out with a pitcher of water, and Janet caught him squarely in the stomach with her outstretched plate. Food and water exploded over both of them; the plate went crashing to the floor.

The boy, red-faced and appalled, tried to brush some of the mess off Janet with his towel. "I — I'm sorry, madam — let me —"

"You can keep your hands to yourself! And tell the cook to fix me a hamburger, if any of you nincompoops know how to cook decent food. You'll get the bill for new clothes."

She stalked out of the room, bits of meat and onion caught in her hair and clinging to her sweater. Utter silence remained in her wake, broken only by the sounds of the distraught waiter trying to clean up the mess.

Teresa was the first to speak. "That," she said in a ringing voice, "was inexcusable." She left her seat and went into the kitchen, returning with a damp cloth and a basin, and began to help. The waiter tried to stop her.

"No, madam, let me — you can't —"

Teresa glared at him. "This wasn't your fault. There's no reason you should have to do all the work. You'd better change into a clean jacket. That one's hopeless." She knelt to her task, avoiding bits of broken crockery.

The rest of us were pushing food around on our plates and trying not to look at each other when Hester made her appearance. Her face was white, though whether with anger or apprehension, I couldn't tell.

"I'm quite sorry dinner was not to your liking," she said, her voice shaking a little. Anger, then, I thought. "Would anyone else like something special prepared?"

"No," said Grace, quietly but firmly. "The haggis is delicious. We're all enjoying it. Aren't we?" She gave the rest of her group an imperious look, and there was a hurried murmur of agreement. I saw Hattie Mae and Jake each take a large mouthful; Chris shoved a little mound under a pile of carrots.

Grace went on. "I feel we should apologize for Miss Douglas's behavior, Mrs. Campbell. I hope you understand that your waiter is in no way to blame. The incident was entirely Janet's fault, although I'm sure she didn't intend to be disruptive."

That was a whole lot more than I was sure of, but presumably Grace knew Janet better than I did.

"Janet has not been herself this week. I believe she is dealing with a personal problem. I hope we can all forget this matter when she returns."

Some hope! But it was a clear directive and the others, as usual when Grace laid down an edict, seemed prepared to submit. As for me, I was glad I was moving away from the contention, though it would make trying to find out anything about Bob's death somewhat awkward. At least Janet's behavior had given me a few things to think about. I hurried through the rest of my meal, wolfing down an apple dumpling without really tasting it, and left the dining room before Janet could get back from changing her clothes.

Hester was still busy in the kitchen, but Andrew had my bill ready. He handed it over with the twinkle very much evident in his eye.

"Still thinking you're going to miss the Iona Hotel, are you?"

"There are aspects I won't miss. After a scene like that, I admit I'm glad you haven't told them yet about the storm coming, and the police, and all."

Andrew looked me straight in the eye and lowered his voice. "Why, Mrs. Martin, I can't imagine what storm you're talking about. Thank you for staying with us, and I hope you'll feel free to book dinner here so long as you're on the island. " He shook my hand, smiled blandly, and excused himself.

So he'd told them the police were coming, but apparently didn't intend to tell them about the weather. I wondered if that decision had been made before or after Janet's little tantrum. Should I drop a hint in Jake's ear, or Grace's? They seemed the most sensible of the party, and might be able to keep the rest from exploding.

On the other hand, since I still had no idea who was on the side of the angels and who wasn't, maybe the best idea was to mind my own business, at least until I could talk to Alan. I fished in my purse for my flashlight, slipped out the door without saying goodbye to anyone, and made my way home through the deep darkness.

Once safely inside my door, I found that,

most unexpectedly, an odd shyness had taken possession of me. Did I really have the nerve to try to call Alan at his conference?

Well, why not? The worst that could happen was that he'd be out and I'd have to leave a message.

I'm not much good at languages, but surely most people in a cosmopolitan city like Brussels would speak English. Although why we should expect them to, when we make no attempt to learn their language . . . what arrogance! Anyway, assuming it was an hour later in Belgium, which I thought was about right, Alan ought to be just getting back from dinner himself.

The operator in the hotel in Brussels, once I had remembered its name and obtained its number, spoke better English than I do. So much for my American prejudices.

"I believe Chief Constable Nesbitt is out at the moment, madam, but I will ring his room."

There was a frustrating interval before the operator spoke again.

"There is no answer, madam. I have checked the conference schedule, and he would be chairing a dinner meeting just now. May I take a message?"

"Oh. Well. No, it's nothing important, really."

"I'm sure he'll want to know who rang."

"Um — you can tell him Dorothy called, but I'll try to call back."

"Thank you, madam. According to the schedule, he has a full day until six o'clock tomorrow, but of course I have no way of knowing his plans for the evening."

"Of course not. Thank you."

I hung up the phone bleakly, and thought about Alan's plans for tomorrow evening. At a glittering hotel in a big city. Dinner, dancing — could he dance? We'd never done that. A concert, perhaps. While I would be sitting around wondering who might be a murderer.

Why couldn't he ever stay close to the phone?

Now that was unfair. He wasn't out carousing tonight; he was working. What could he do, anyway? He couldn't solve my problem for me, and, in any case, I could hardly give him details over the phone. In fact, there was no point at all in talking to him.

That made me feel even lonelier.

I wandered around my tiny domain, looked at an old copy of *Country Life* someone had left in the living room, and wished, uncharacteristically, that the owners of the cottage had seen fit to equip it with a television. Oh, well, the reception would probably be awful in this remote part of the world. They might at least have had the forethought to provide a decent selection of reading material. I wondered whatever had possessed me to come to a place like this, anyway, all by myself, with nothing to do, no one to talk to, not even a cat . . .

Oh, for heaven's sake! And what would a cat have done for the last two days while I had myself locked out like a simpleton? In a thoroughly bad temper I double-locked the doors, turned out the lights, and went to bed.

In the morning, as is the way of mornings, things looked better. True, the weather was deteriorating, if the gathering clouds were any indication, but it wasn't yet threatening; the wind was no more than one might expect on any autumn day. Perhaps the ferry would be running today, and the police would get here early, and they would decide Bob's death was an unfortunate accident, and the Chicago contingent could get off the island and on their way home. Perhaps I'd hear from Tom and Lynn. Perhaps Alan would call.

Well, no, he wouldn't, would he? — since I hadn't given his hotel my phone number. I debated calling them again and decided against it. Probably the same operator wouldn't be on duty, but after refusing to leave a message last night, I certainly didn't want to seem like — no, I wouldn't call.

But I could call Jane. I should, in fact. Why hadn't I thought of that last night?

Because I was too busy feeling sorry for myself, that was why. Self-pity has the most devastating effect on common sense.

Jane answered on the first ring.

"I got your letter, Jane, and the key. Thanks so much for all your trouble. I'm settled in, and I love the cottage, it's tiny and cute and —"

"Are you all right?"

"What do you mean? Of course I'm all right. For heaven's sake, it was only an accident! I'm sure it was an accident. Why does everybody think, every time I'm incidentally involved, it has to be a murder?"

There was a long pause at the other end of the line.

"Oh," I said in a subdued tone. "What were you talking about?"

"Never mind what I was talking about. What are you?"

"Nothing that matters. I mean, it does, of course, but surely not much to me. Someone I didn't know died — fell off the cliff in Fingal's Cave — and I saw it happen.

And it had to have been an accident. Anything else is — let's start over. Why did you want to know if I was all right?"

"Weather. Mother and father of all storms headed straight for you. Hatches battened?"

"Well, I think the cottage is reasonably weather-tight. The roof seems to be sound, and so on."

"Hmmm."

"I can't imagine what you're worried about. The weather's perfectly ordinary. It'll probably rain later on, but what else is new? This is the UK. Let me give you my phone number, just in case." I recited it to her. "How are the cats?"

"As usual. Sure you're going to be ready for the storm? "

She made it sound like a full-fledged typhoon. "Of course. Look, this line isn't very good and I need to make another call. I'll call you again tomorrow."

I hung up before she could worry some more. That was unlike Jane; there must be something on her mind.

I had deliberately downplayed the weather forecast to my worried friend, but I'd better play it straight with the Andersons. They were planning to arrive in a couple of days, after all, and they needed to know what they were getting into.

". . . please leave a message at the tone."

Of all the infuriating devices the twentieth century has spawned, the answering machine must be one of the worst. When I make a call, it's because I want to talk to somebody, and to be greeted by that somebody's mechanized voice is maddening. And I invariably spend the first few seconds casting imprecations at the machine instead of composing my own message, so that I then waste some of my allotted time stammering.

"Umm . . . this is Dorothy, and — oh, for goodness' sake, I hope you're not on your way to Scotland! Because I'm calling to tell you not to come. I mean — not right away. Because there's a storm coming, and you might not be able to get here anyway. Oh, I can't talk on one of these things, just call me if you get this before you leave London."

I left the number and hung up, and immediately felt a pang of guilt because I hadn't inquired after Tom. I had assumed they'd already left for the trip north, but it was really too soon for that. What if Tom had had a relapse, and was in the hospital? Or — worse?

I called back.

"Lynn, do call me right away, will you? Sorry to bother you twice, but I wasn't very coherent before. I hope everything's all right."

That wasn't much better than the first message. Thoroughly annoyed with myself, I burned some toast on the unfamiliar grill, overcooked the oatmeal to a sodden mass, and threw it all away in a fine temper. Unlike the great chefs (or so their reputation has it), I can't cook when I'm in a snit.

I was certainly having a good time all by myself, wasn't I?

There was, I reminded myself, a cafe in the village. Presumably they served breakfast. If not, one of the shops might run to scones. I prudently put on my raincoat, picked up my purse (making sure the key was in it), and stalked off.

10

I had a very good breakfast, at a very reasonable price, at the little cafe with the imposing name of Martyr's Bay Restaurant, and left feeling more like myself. It is humbling to realize how much one's emotions are ruled by the state of one's stomach.

It was a glorious day, for anyone who doesn't absolutely require sunshine. After more than a year of living in England, I've learned to appreciate weather in many of its less placid varieties. Today was decidedly chilly, and the wind had picked up a bit, sending the clouds scudding. I was blown up the road rather briskly myself, glad my bright little tam was close fitting. A wide-brimmed hat would have sailed to Loch Lomond by noon.

I got back to my cottage in record time, bowled along by the wind, but I was too exhilarated to go inside. This was Scotland the way I had expected it to be, and I wasn't going to waste time moping indoors or pondering horrors. I went on up the road; it had looked like a private drive once you got past my house, but I decided that it might not be, and, in any case, I wasn't going to do any harm. Iona seemed the sort of place where, so long as you shut the gates behind you and kept out of people's crops, nobody would pay much attention to you.

There wasn't anything very exciting along the road, which had disintegrated into a track, except one rather odd-looking three-gabled house on the right. Still, I hadn't explored this part of the island; I might find a shortcut to the Abbey.

When I came to the gate of the house, I stopped in surprise. The signpost in front referred to the Bishop's House, but there was also a small notice board with the shield of the Episcopal Church, the name St. Columba's Chapel, and a listing of service times. The place was evidently a church, and of my own kind at that. I boldly opened the gate and went up to the door. There was a faded sign saying that the church was always open for prayer, so I lifted the latch and went in.

I was in a little hallway with doors to either side and one straight ahead. Voices and cooking smells came from somewhere, but no humans were in sight, so I walked through and opened the door in front of me.

I found myself in a minute chapel, a doll

house of a chapel. Made of stone and virtually unadorned, it could probably, in a pinch, seat a dozen people on its hard, upright wooden chairs. Scotland's prevailing Calvinism was apparent even here; there was an austerity that spoke of sternly puritan influences.

But the kneelers were padded, and I sank to my knees in gratitude. Here was rest and peace. I could pray for Bob, and those who mourned him, for Jake, for my other unhappy countrymen at the hotel, and, indeed, for myself, my worries and fears.

Some time later the door behind me opened quietly, and someone came in. I stood to go, bowed to the altar, and turned to find an elderly, rather stooped, but kindly-looking man in thick glasses and a clerical collar.

"Good morning. I didn't mean to disturb you."

His accent was English; I figured he hadn't been on Iona long. "Good morning. You didn't; I was just about to leave anyway. You're the rector here?"

"The vicar, yes. And you'd be the American lady staying in Dove Cottage. Our neighbor, in fact."

The hat again! "Dorothy Martin." I shook his hand. "I'm doing a little exploring today. Is there a way to the Abbey from here?"

162

"Yes, indeed, follow the footpath to the gate on your left, and it's straight up. You will remember to shut the gates, won't you? The Abbey grazes sheep in that field."

"I'll remember, and thank you, Father . . . ?"

"Pym, and 'Mister' will be splendid. We're quite low church here. And now, if you will excuse me, I must see if anything can be done about patching our leak before the next storm does some real damage."

He looked ruefully over the tops of his glasses at the ceiling of the little church where, I noticed for the first time, a large damp spot was spreading.

"I'll leave you to it, then. Good luck!"

The wind was perhaps even stronger when I left the shelter of the little church, but no rain had yet made its appearance, so I decided to go on up. I had given the Abbey short shrift so far, and it was, after all, the principal tourist attraction on Iona.

I enjoyed the brief walk. I have always lived in towns, and the charm of a country footpath is still new to me. Especially to an American, used to our rather paranoid views about private property, the idea that these public rights-of-way had existed for centuries and could not, by law, be closed off or destroyed had a great deal of appeal. Scottish law might be different, but I knew that in some parts of England a footpath couldn't be fenced off or otherwise barricaded unless the landowner could prove that no one had used it for the last hundred years! What a delightful thought.

So I closed the gates carefully behind me, avoided the hazards of a field full of sheep as best I might, and duty arrived at the Abbey.

It was, I admitted, an imposing structure. A great deal of it was modern rebuilding, but the side I was approaching was medieval, at least as to the walls; all of the roofs had fallen in over time and were rebuilt in the twentieth century. Here at the back of the church the sense of the ancient, the feeling of worship carried on for nearly fifteen hundred years, was far stronger for me than inside the building. I lingered for a bit, touching the moss and lichens on the stone walls and dreaming about monks long dead. I even leaned against the old stone wall, in part for shelter from the wind, but in part, I admitted to myself, to try to absorb some of the past I love so much.

Unfortunately, as I leaned I looked out over the Sound of Iona, and watched the little ferry from Mull arrive at the jetty. So it was running again, and that meant . . . I watched as a car drove off the boat.

A police car.

With a resentful sigh, I turned around and headed for the road and the Iona Hotel.

The first person I met in the hall was Jake. "There's good news and bad news," he said with a trace of a twinkle back in his voice.

"Okay, I'll bite." He seemed to have gotten over his embarrassment about telling me his life story.

"The good news, I guess, is that the cops are on their way, so we'll get that business out of the way pretty soon."

"Yes, I saw them drive off the ferry; that's why I'm here. And the bad news?"

"The bad news is that a storm is also on its way."

"Oh?" I tried my best to look surprised. "A bad one?"

Jake looked at me closely. "Yeah, well, I guess you knew that already, too, huh?"

"Well — I had heard a weather forecast, but I'm honestly not sure I believe it. I mean, look at the weather now. A little windy, and it's going to rain, but nothing out of the ordinary."

"Yeah. Anyway, we're leaving today by the two-thirty ferry, so we don't get caught by the storm. So how about climbing that hill with me before lunch? You know, Dun Eye?"

"Dun Ee, they pronounce it, I think. I

thought you climbed it yesterday afternoon."

"Nah, I waited while everybody else did. It didn't look too bad, but I was tired already. They did say there was a terrific view, and I thought we could talk. And I could apologize."

"You've nothing to apologize for," I said warmly.

"Yeah, well. So what about it? You look kind of stiff — can't let your muscles seize up, y'know."

I didn't really want to climb a mountain, or even a little hill, which is all Dun I really is. And it wasn't wise to go off alone with anyone, even Jake. On the other hand, would a refusal look funny? Or would it hurt his feelings? And it would be a good chance to talk to him, but didn't I already know his background pretty well? Anyway, if they were all leaving, my suspicions would forever remain academic.

"Well — I suppose —" I had begun, when Andrew came into the hall, very formal, a little tense.

"Mrs. Martin, Mr. Goldstein, would you come into the lounge, please? The police have arrived."

The other five guests were seated when we walked into the room. None of them looked at us. None of them said anything.

"Ah, good," said the taller of the two men who were standing. He was wearing a suit and tie; his pepper-and-salt hair was cut rather short, and he had a brisk, businesslike way about him. The other man wore a black uniform and had removed his cap with the black-and-white-checked band. He looked younger and carried a notebook.

"You must be Mrs. Dorothy Martin and Mr. Jacob Goldstein, am I right? I'm Detective Inspector MacLean, from the Strathclyde Police, and I need to ask everyone a few more questions about the unfortunate mishap that befell Mr. — Williams, is it? If you'd just be seated, please."

We sat, silently. I took a deep breath and told myself to be careful. This could be tricky. I jumped when the inspector addressed me.

"Mrs. Martin."

"Yes?" It came out as a squeak. I cleared my throat.

"I understand you were the only witness to Mr. Williams's fall. Is that right?"

"Yes, we were alone in the cave at the time." I had my voice under control. Now if there were just something I could do about my breathing.

"Could you tell me how that came to be

the case? Mr. MacPherson tells me a fair-sized party was visiting Staffa that afternoon."

"Yes, but the others were all a lot quicker on their feet than I was." This part was easy. "I have bad knees, and the stairs and stepping stones were hard going for me; I had to take them slowly. By the time I decided I was going to the cave rather than the top of the island, almost everyone else was already coming back, and so when I got to the cave I thought for a moment I was the only one there. It was only when I got well inside that I saw Bob — Mr. Williams."

"Ah. You knew him well, then?"

"I didn't know him at all, except to speak to. Americans tend to exchange first names on short acquaintance, Inspector."

"I see. Please continue, Mrs. Martin."

I went through it as briefly as I could.

"And you are quite sure there was no one near him, besides you?"

"There was no one near him, period; there was a good twenty feet between us, and we were quite alone."

"Ah, yes." There was a pause. "You travel on an American passport, Mrs. Martin, but you give your address as Sherebury, Belleshire?"

"Yes, I've lived there for over a year now.

I've taken no steps to become a British subject; I don't even know how you do that, and I'm not ready to relinquish my American citizenship. If you want a reference in Sherebury, you might contact Chief Constable Alan Nesbitt. He's in Brussels just now, however."

"Yes, we have heard from Mr. Nesbitt."

I looked up sharply. This was a totally unexpected development. "May I ask — in what connection?"

"In connection with this inquiry." The inspector's tone was bland.

"But — this is Scotland, he has no jurisdiction —"

"Precisely, madam. And may I ask how you know the distinguished chief constable?"

"In connection with another inquiry." I became equally bland; the inspector annoyed me. However, I'd better establish my credibility. "I had occasion, quite accidentally, to help him with one or two troubling matters in Sherebury, and we became friends." And if that wasn't quite accurate, it was close enough. My exact relationship with Alan was none of his, or anybody else's, business.

"I see. Thank you, Mrs. Martin. I believe that's all."

I rose. "May I be excused, then?"

"Just a few minutes more, if you don't mind."

I sat back down again.

Inspector MacLean went through all the routine questions with everyone in the room. He learned exactly nothing, so far as I could tell. Everyone had been elsewhere, had seen nothing. They had noticed nothing unusual in Bob's behavior; he had been, perhaps, a little moody, but he was often moody. In short, their evidence agreed exactly with what I had so carefully said. Nobody mentioned the wet rocks. It was obvious that they thought he was making a great deal of fuss over nothing, and obvious, too, that they blamed me for their ordeal. If you hadn't been there, their looks seemed to say, if you didn't have important friends in the police, friends you never told us about . . .

"Has anyone anything to add?" he asked finally. I thought he looked especially hard at me. I smiled at him and kept my lips firmly shut. Later, if I could speak to him privately . . . but just now I wanted urgently to get out of the room before their anger could be unleashed upon me.

"Very well," the inspector said at last, when his apparently pointless questioning

170

had ground to a halt. "You are entitled to know that the search for Mr. Williams's body has so far been fruitless. It is continuing today, and will continue, as weather permits, until the body is found or the search is abandoned as useless." He paused for a moment, appeared to make a decision, and continued. "It appears that Mr. Williams's death was an unfortunate accident, and that is the way I shall report it to my superiors. Unless you wish to wait for the recovery of the body, which I must tell you is problematic at best, you are free to leave when you wish. Of course, if anyone recalls anything further about the matter, you are welcome to ring me in Oban." He gave us a phone number, bowed slightly, and left, his unnamed assistant in tow.

"And that's that," said Chris in an oddly satisfied tone of voice. "I was afraid they might make us stick around."

"They could hardly have done that," said Grace, as cool as ever. "We were merely witnesses, at second hand, to an accident. Mrs. Martin, perhaps, but even then . . ."

She looked at me and I seized my chance. "Yes, well, I'm glad you're getting to leave before the storm. It was — nice meeting all of you. Excuse me, I left something in the oven."

I escaped, waiting until I was out of sight of the hotel before breaking into an unpracticed run.

The police were in a car, of course, and got to the jetty long before I did, but the ferry wasn't there yet. I caught up with them, breathless, and knocked on the car window.

"Inspector, there is something else. I didn't want to tell you in front of the others."

He looked annoyed, but stepped out of the car. "Yes, Mrs. Martin?"

I told them about the water. I had the sense not to go into theories of what it might mean.

"Indeed. You were how far away from Mr. Williams?"

"Twenty feet or so, I suppose. I'm not good at estimating distances."

"No. And you say it was dark in the cave?"

"Well — there was a cloud over the sun just then. It was darkish, but —"

"And you did not examine the path at any time to determine whether it was, indeed, wet?"

"Of course not! I had to try to get help —"

"Certainly. Pity, though. Because none of the others mentioned it, and, of course, there is now no way to know, is there?"

His manner was condescending. I glared at him, unable to find a response.

"Ah, the ferry has arrived. Thank you, Mrs. Martin, for being so conscientious, but I think if you search your memory, you will find that you were deceived by a trick of the light. Good afternoon!"

He sat back down in the car, and I watched as the car drove onto the ferry. The hatch was slow about closing, sticking a few times, and I had the crazy idea of running aboard and trying to make my point, but then the hatch was secured, and with a series of toots, the ferry was off.

With it went my only hope of advice or support.

11

I got to my cottage the minute I could and tried to call Alan. Of course he was in a meeting. I left an urgent message for him and sank onto a chair at the kitchen table, my head in my hands.

I'd cast away my lifeline, in the shape of Inspector MacLean — or perhaps he'd dropped it. I knew, of course, why he'd paid no attention to me. Even though my information was vague in the extreme, a good policeman would still have listened, if he hadn't already been prejudiced against me. He'd snubbed me because he wasn't about to be given advice by some English policeman.

Why *was* Alan having conversations with the police in Oban? I didn't understand the exact relationship between England and Scotland, but I did know that their laws are different and their constabularies separate. An English chief constable has, in Scotland, no authority whatever.

Well, when Alan called back, he could tell me what was going on. And phone lines be damned, he could also tell me what to do. I'd tried to involve the Strathclyde police. Since they weren't interested, I needed some sound advice, and Alan was just the man.

For the truth was, I was still far from sure that murder was anything more than a figment of my imagination. Everything I had seen, and it was little enough, could have an innocent as well as a sinister explanation. Nor had I made any startling revelations in the course of my (admittedly unsystematic) poking around. Most of the Americans were simply nice enough people with eccentricities. Janet, to be sure, had revealed herself in unpleasant colors over dinner last night, but a closed mind and a hot temper don't necessarily add up to murder.

My chair was getting very hard; I got up and paced. I knew why I was getting nowhere. Despite all my pep talks to myself, I was tiptoeing around the genuine questions, avoiding any real, organized investigation, because I didn't want any of these people to be guilty of murder. However I might feel about any of them individually, they were my all fellow countrymen and -women, and I felt like Judas.

Very well, said my inner critic. *You don't want to prove one of them guilty. Try to prove them innocent.*

It's extremely hard to prove a negative, I thought doubtfully, wanting to be convinced.

We're not talking hard evidence here, for a court of law. You want to know, in your own mind, that none of them killed Bob. Any of them could have done it, so what you have to do is satisfy yourself that none of them had any motive, and you can stop being afraid of them, or worried about trouble with the police.

I have often had occasion to be very annoyed with my self-critical side, which seems to spend its time keeping me from having any fun and prodding me into doing things I don't want to do. This time I hugged myself, by way of thankfulness. Prove they *didn't* do it! Hallelujah, what a wonderful idea! That one I could approach with enthusiasm.

It would be easier, I thought as I sat back down, if I had a friend on Iona to help me think. Even a cat on my lap would have helped. A warm, purring cat aids my thought processes considerably. But failing any assistance, I'd have to do the best I could alone.

I had just pulled the phone pad to me — I love to make lists — when there was a tap at the door.

"You forgot, didn't you?"

It was Jake. I opened the door wider and racked my brains. "Forgot . . . "

"We're climbing Dun I."

I had forgotten, totally, and, in fact, I'd never really promised. "Oh, but Jake, the weather! The wind! And it's going to rain any minute. Don't you think we should put it off for another time?"

"Not doing anything but blowing. Up at the hotel they say the rain'll hold off for another four, five hours, and the hill only takes an hour or so. And there won't be another time for me, because we're leaving later, remember? What do you say?"

"Well —"

"Good. You ready to go?"

I wasn't, actually. I wanted some thinking time. I also wanted to wait for the phone to ring. Surely Alan got some time off, at least for meals!

But since he hadn't called yet, he probably wouldn't until lunch. In which case, the sooner I left the better, so as to be back early. I speculated briefly about any possible danger, remembered I had decided not to think negatively and anyway this would be a good chance to ask Jake some pointed questions, and smiled at him. If it was a little forced, I hoped he wouldn't notice.

"As ready as I'll ever be, I suppose. I'll get

my waterproof jacket, just in case."

Equipped with walking sticks someone had left in my umbrella stand, we set off.

"There's a shortcut if you go this way." Jake pointed. "I wandered around the Abbey grounds yesterday while everybody else was killing themselves on that hill, and found it."

I didn't tell him I knew the shortcut, too. I was actually rather fond of Jake. We turned left out of Dove Cottage, walked past the Bishop's House, and took the footpath to the Abbey.

"See?" said Jake as proudly as if he'd discovered a new country.

"Well done. That probably saved us half a mile or so. But, Jake," I went on as we walked past the Abbey up toward the road, "why are we doing this at all? The wind is getting stronger all the time, the rain is coming, it's as cold as November. Why are you so hell-bent on climbing a hill that's probably a great deal like other hills?"

"I'm not. The hill's an excuse."

"Good grief, for what?" My fears and suspicions rose again, in spite of myself, and I planted both feet on the path and refused to move.

"I wanted to talk to you. It's warmer if you keep walking."

He trudged steadily on and I was forced

to follow or be left behind.

"What about?"

"Aaron. Unless you're tired of hearing my sob stories."

"Of course not!" That put a whole different spin on it. I couldn't try to question Jake when he needed a listener. There are limits to even my nosiness. "I just didn't want to refer to it myself, if it was going to make you unhappy. I could see you wanted to drop the subject yesterday."

"Yeah. I don't talk about it much, but you're an easy lady to talk to, y'know?"

I just smiled, and we proceeded in amiable silence. We had left the Abbey grounds and were heading up the road, north toward the end of the island.

"How far is it?"

"The hill's over there, but we have to go almost beyond it to where there's a path. It's probably no more than — oh, say, half a mile to the top. You tired?"

"Not yet. This part's easy."

The wind was blowing steadily from our left, but it didn't impede our progress much. In fact, it was rather exhilarating.

"My word, look over there!" I pointed to the farm we were passing. "Isn't that Janet in front of the house, arguing with that farmer?"

It was certainly Janet, and "arguing" was a mild term for her conversation. She was shouting, her arms waving in the face of the man I assumed was a farmer. He looked rather bewildered, and didn't seem to be saying much. The house was set well back from the road, so we couldn't hear what Janet was saying, only the angry tone of her voice, though the wind flung us a word now and again.

"You're lying!" was one intriguing little snatch we caught, and "I'll find out . . . sorry you ever . . ."

We passed out of earshot.

"Now what on earth was that all about?" I demanded.

Jake shrugged. "She has a temper, and she hates the Scots."

"Then why did she come to Scotland?"

He shrugged again and we plodded on.

"So tell me about Aaron," I said after a few minutes, hoping I wasn't rushing Jake.

"It would have been his birthday," he said slowly, helping me over a cattle grid, "today. He would have been sixteen. I was gonna get him a car. I had it all planned out. Driving lessons, and then I'd show him the fine points — city driving, expressway driving, how to spot the crazies — and then I'd turn him loose. Can't keep them babies forever, y'know."

I wanted to hug him, or offer him some of the consolation my own faith offered, but all he wanted right then was to talk about it, poor man. I wondered who'd been around to help him mourn when the boy died. No wife, no daughter, a son-in-law who wanted no part of his child — it must have been terribly lonely.

"Jake, how did it happen? A blood transfusion?"

"I don't know."

I thought he was going to leave it at that, but after a long pause he went on.

"He never even told me he had it. The city clinic will give anybody over twelve the test. The first I knew about it, he was dead. He left a note . . ."

He couldn't continue, so we toiled on in silence. We had passed a couple of farms before Jake pointed out a gate on the left.

"This is the one. Are you still game?"

"We've come this far. I admit I'm loath to leave Iona without getting to the top of Dun I. It's one of the required things, isn't it?"

There was no path from here. We ambled across a field where sheep were grazing placidly. They were annoyed at our invasion, but not especially frightened. I suppose even sheep, stupid as they are, can get used to tourists.

The field was marshy, and the walking

sticks were a boon. "I'm going to have to scrape pounds of mud off these when we get back," I commented, grabbing Jake's arm to keep from sinking ankle-deep in one deceptive patch of grassy mud.

"Better that than having to pull each other out."

"Easier, too. I can just picture . . ." I giggled, and I was glad to see Jake smile again.

The going got really rough when we left the field. There was a sort of track leading up the mountain, as I was beginning to think of it. I'm sure the young and fit would have found the climb a mere stroll, but I was panting after five minutes, and my knees were complaining bitterly. I tried not to think of Jake's heart condition.

We made it, though. We were both flat beat, but we stood for a triumphant moment at the summit, leaning into the wind that up here was almost strong enough to knock us down, before Jake dropped to a large rock and I collapsed next to him.

"That was a damn-fool thing to do," he said presently.

"Yes." I stretched contentedly. "I'm glad we did it. Are you going to put a stone on the cairn?"

"You better believe it. Later."

"Yes."

We sat there, the wind blowing right through us, and let our lungs and hearts get back to normal. I looked at the cairn, the pile of small stones built up over the years by climbers who had wanted to commemorate their accomplishment. It was close to the pointed stone column that marked the highest point on the island and also, I had been told, served as a triangulation point for map makers and others interested in such esoteric stuff.

"You can see Staffa." Jake pointed.

"So you can. It looks kind of like a ship from here, doesn't it? That would be the bow, there on the left, where it rises."

"D'you mind looking at it?"

"Not from here. I might get a little queasy if I had to go back in the cave."

"You really didn't see anything? I thought you were being kind of cagey with that cop."

Uh-oh. If Jake realized I'd left something out, maybe the others had, too. I laughed, and hoped the laughter sounded more genuine to Jake than it did to me. "I just resented being treated like a suspect. I've actually been involved in a couple of murder cases in Shrebury, where I live — happened on to them, innocent bystander sort of thing — and the police there know me pretty well. Well, you'll have gathered that. I guess I've gotten used to being treated with a little more respect. Gotten spoiled, in other words. Besides, it was obviously an accident — or just possibly suicide, although I don't think so. He fell, he didn't jump. And what does it matter which it was? Except for the state of his soul, and that's between him and God, anyway."

"Umm."

It was an equivocal sort of noise, and I remembered that Jake didn't believe in God, but he said no more, so perhaps I'd diverted him.

We sat for a few minutes more and listened to the howl of the wind. I watched the boats in the Sound. I could see none that were going anywhere; a few sailboats and launches were riding at anchor, tossed madly by the waves that were rising by the minute.

"Shall we go down?" I said finally. "I'm freezing, and starving, and that rain's coming, sure as Christmas."

"Right." Jake heaved himself to his feet, helped me up, and after we had each found a stone we liked and ceremoniously balanced it atop the cairn, we stood, leaning into the wind, looking down at the island.

"Jake!" I said suddenly. "I've been watching the Sound for a good fifteen minutes now. Doesn't the ferry make a roundtrip every twenty or so?"

"Something like that, I guess."

"Well, I haven't seen it. Nothing's moving down there. Look, it isn't crossing, and I can't see it at either jetty."

He put his hand up to his eyes and squinted. "You're right. Maybe we should go find out what's up, huh?" We slipped and slid our way back down to the road, and hurried as fast as we could to the jetty.

No one was there. No one was waiting for the ferry, or mending nets. There were no wagons ready for tourists. The nerve center of the village was deserted.

Jake was the one who spotted the piece of paper. Handwritten in pencil, it was attached to a piling, and was flapping madly in the wind. "Notice," it read. "Iona ferry out of order. Back in service soon."

"What does that mean?" asked Jake blankly. " 'Soon.' When's soon?"

"What I think it means," I said grimly, "is that you're going to miss your plane on Saturday. I was going to invite you to lunch, but maybe you'd better go up and tell the others."

I made it home just before the rain started pelting down. The blue-black sky made it look like early evening, though it was just past noon. I decided I would put a stew in a slow oven to cook for dinner before I fixed myself a little lunch. Then I could consider my problem.

So when I'd eaten some mulligatawny soup and cleaned up the kitchen, I sat down with my pad in front of me. All right, start with the victim. That was always Hercule Poirot's approach, and who am I to question the masters? What did I remember about Bob Williams, alive and dead?

Actually, he wasn't a very memorable person. I had rather disliked him, but not passionately; he didn't have a strong enough personality to inspire any sort of passion in anybody, it seemed to me. And that was apparently the way his fellow travelers viewed him, too. Most of them found him a nuisance, and ineffectual, but well-meaning enough. Grace had expressed some respect for his work, as had Teresa. I didn't recall that Janet or Chris had said a word about him.

Very well, then, what had I noticed about his state of mind? Had he appeared suicidal? Shamefully, I brightened at the thought.

Certainly he had been moody the day he'd died. He'd spent at least part of the day alone; I'd seen him walking at the north end of the island without another soul in sight, and later on the boat he'd sat by himself. But people, I reluctantly admitted, can be solitary without planning to kill themselves.

No, I was forced to agree with the Chicagoans, who were certain he hadn't killed himself.

Wait a minute! If one of them had killed him, wouldn't the murderer, at any rate, be pushing the suicide theory? Since nobody was doing that, didn't that mean that I could relax and forget about murder?

Unless, of course, whoever it was had decided to let me take the blame. I had been alone with the man, after all. Although, if that tantalizing flicker of something at the entrance to the cave had been anything more than my imagination, it might have been someone who could vindicate me. Or, of course, it might have been the murderer, who would have no interest in testifying on my behalf.

That was thinking negatively again. It wasn't murder, I reminded myself. That's the hypothesis du jour. Stick to it and stop chasing stray ideas.

Definitely, I needed a cat. Cats excel at reminding humans of the realities of life. They do not let their people go off on tangents. Imagined horrors always take a backseat to the needs of cats.

I got up to stir the stew, and heard a sound at the back door that I thought wasn't the wind.

It was probably the savory smell of the stew that had brought Stan to my kitchen door, standing up on his hind legs and tapping with his front paws, demanding admittance.

"Well! Might have known you'd turn up too late to be useful. Where were you when I needed you?"

Stan replied by twining himself around my ankles and walking pointedly over to the stove.

"It isn't ready yet. And the leftover soup is pretty spicy. But I have some cheese I'd be glad to share."

I ended up having some myself, with oat cakes, and giving Stan a little of the soup he insisted he wanted (and finished, to the last drop). He also wanted my shortbread (he had hopped up to the counter and discovered the box), but I finally drew the line. "Look here, old boy, neither of us needs all that butter and sugar. You go chase some mice or rabbits or whatever, work off some of your lunch, and maybe by tea time I'll relent."

I had to shove him out the door, but he had cheered me considerably, even if he hadn't aided my mental processes. I decided it was time for an afternoon nap. I was becoming addicted to them, something about all the fresh air, I told myself. When I woke, since I was apparently stuck on this island with the Chicago crew, I really would work out a systematic approach to clearing them all of murder.

12

I was awakened by a howl of wind so loud and angry that it penetrated closed windows, and rain that struck the house like hailstones. I rushed, disheveled and disoriented, to close the kitchen window, and when I stubbed my toe on an inconvenient footstool and tried to turn on the lights, I discovered that the electricity had gone out.

It wasn't entirely dark, but very nearly. I peered at my watch and finally made out the time to be almost five, much later than I had intended to sleep. Oh, dear, what was going to happen to my dinner in an electric oven?

The thought made me hungry, and I was also thirsty; a cup of tea would be very welcome.

The teakettle was electric.

Glumly, I drank a glass of water, nibbled on a piece of the shortbread I had intended to share with Stan, and considered my options.

I had no idea whether my electrical problem was only mine. It could be spread over the whole island, if something had happened to the underwater cable that carried the supply from Mull. One glance out the window had assured me that lights could have been burning in every other building on Iona, and I wouldn't have seen them; the rain resembled Niagara Falls and cut off visibility completely.

Nor could I estimate how long it might be before my service was restored, though certainly it would have to wait until the rain had stopped. No repairman in his senses would work on electric lines with this much water in the air, or at any rate, he wouldn't work on them long.

What a grim thought! What I needed was a bit of cheer. Like a phone call from Alan.

He ought to have called by now, surely. If it was six in Belgium, he must be back at the hotel.

Maybe they'd forgotten to give him the message. Or — well, I was past caring whether he thought I was being a pest. I badly needed to hear Alan's voice. After I'd talked to him I'd call the Iona Hotel and find out if they had any way to cook and could accommodate me for dinner. I picked up the phone.

It was dead.

It was at that moment that I felt the first stab of real fear.

I was alone and isolated, in the middle of a storm on a small and vulnerable island, an island that, perhaps, harbored a murderer.

No! No, it doesn't. No murderer. Certainly not.

I put the receiver back on the cradle, slowly, quietly. The sounds of the storm intensified, took on a keening, human quality. Something, a tree limb probably, was thumping on the front of the house, and the sound rasped at my nerves.

Especially when I remembered that there were no trees at the front of the house.

I crept out of the kitchen into the tiny hall, my heart pounding, my fear growing, and tried to peer out the window of the front door. Something obscured what little view there was, something dark . . .

. . . that shouted my name in a Scottish accent.

I eased the door open, pushing hard against the fierce blast that tried to tear it out of my hands. Andrew Campbell stood in the doorway, dripping wet, his legs braced against the force of the gale.

"Mrs. Martin," he shouted, "the electricity is out on the whole island, and the phones — the cables have snapped. You'll not be able to cook, you've no light, and there's the worst gale coming we've seen in years. I've sent my staff home, but you'd best come back to the hotel with me."

"But —"

"We've no time to talk; in a wee bit I'll not be able to drive! You'd best gather up what perishable food you have. It'll spoil here, and we have our own generator and proper refrigeration. Or — I'll do that, while you pack up what you'll need for two days. Hurry, woman!"

The last two words told me more than the rest. If Andrew Campbell, a quietly courteous man, felt obliged to issue curt commands, he was seriously worried.

I did as he told me.

That five-minute drive to the hotel rivaled any roller coaster ride for sheer terror. Andrew's little car, buffeted by the howling wind, left the narrow road several times; once I was sure we were going to turn over. The rain was tropical in intensity; I hoped Andrew could see, for I couldn't. I also hoped the screams I kept hearing were only the wind, and not animals in distress.

I had expected to see the hotel beckoning from its hilltop with welcome lights. Surely those could be seen, even through the rain. But my straining eyes saw nothing but rain and darkness until an even darker bulk loomed close to us, and I realized we had pulled up to the back door of the hotel.

Oh, no. No electricity here, either? Their generator had failed?

I saw the answer as I struggled through the door with my groceries. Every window was firmly shuttered. Although a few lights were on inside the house, not a glimmer reached the outside. Nailed shut, I supposed.

It hit me for the first time, then, that this was going to be one doozy of a storm, the like of which I had never seen. Nor, I devoutly hoped, would I ever see its like again.

The tumult was subdued as soon as we were inside. It took both of us to shut the door and bolt it against the manic frenzy of the wind, but the solid oak of doors and shutters created a semblance of peace.

The voices I could hear coming from the lounge, however, weren't peaceful. The natives were restless. I ignored them and went to the kitchen to drop off my groceries.

"Hester, is there anything I can do? It's a big job, running this place without any of your usual help."

"No. I thank you, mind, but Andrew and I have done this before. Storms are not unknown on Iona."

I liked the way she said it, with the dry humor I was beginning to associate with the Scots.

194

"There's always food in the freezer, cooked and ready to serve, some of it. Tonight it's *boeuf bourguignon,* with me not lifting a finger! I'll just ask you to conserve the electricity, though. Andrew will have told you we generate our own in emergencies, but the supply is limited, and we've none too much petrol on hand."

"Of course. I won't turn on any lights. I was just going to take a bath. Is the water heater working?"

Hester beamed. "We're very fortunate. Ours runs on Calor gas, and they brought a new bottle last week. So use all the water you like! Dear knows there'll be enough and to spare in the loch, with this rain."

We'd be lucky, I thought darkly, if the loch didn't overflow and send waterfalls cascading down to flood all Iona. I had the sense to keep my mouth shut.

As I went into the hall, the angry conversation in the lounge seemed even louder.

"But we've *got* to catch our plane! The CRA, stingy misers, told us we had to pay for 'any changes in travel plans.' And I don't know about the rest of you, but I can't afford —"

"Honey, the money's the least of it. I got responsibilities. Who's gonna take the choir to Indianapolis next week? Who's gonna take care of my boys? Who's gonna —"

"This is an utterly pointless discussion. We can hardly be held responsible for the weather. We will I leave this island when we are able to leave. Surely the CRA —"

" 'Go to Iona,' they said. 'Peace and quiet,' they said. I want peace and quiet, I should stand in the middle of Michigan Avenue at rush hour —"

"— never get home, never see my church again, the choir, the organ —"

"It's her fault."

I walked into the room to Janet's accusation. The rest of them stopped talking.

"We could have taken the ferry this morning if she hadn't made us stick around for the cops."

They all looked at me. I stood where I was. I was soaked through and needed a hot bath, but it was time I asserted myself.

"Janet, that's nonsense and you know it. You had no plans to leave today until you knew the storm was coming. No, don't interrupt." It was my best schoolteacher tone, known to quell a roomful of unruly sixthgraders. No one said a word.

"Furthermore, I had nothing whatever to do with the fact that you were required to be questioned. That's standard police procedure. And certainly I didn't cause the breakdown of the ferry. We've all been forced together by the storm. It will be easier if we try to be nice to each other.

"I don't know my Bible nearly as well as Hattie Mae, but I do remember a remark from another source at about the time of the New Testament. I quoted it to Jake when we first met: 'See how these Christians love one another.' I recommend we try it."

And I stalked out.

Andrew had put my suitcase in my same room. I filled the tub, stripped off my wet clothes, and prepared to luxuriate.

It didn't work.

Oh, I got warm, all right, but my taut muscles wouldn't relax. It didn't matter how often I told myself that I was being foolish, that there was no murderer in the building. My mind struggled to believe it, but my nerves stayed tense. Just be careful, something in a hidden layer of my consciousness kept saving. Just watch yourself.

I splooshed out of the tub, put on dry clothes, and plodded down to the lounge.

I wasn't sure how I would be greeted after that remarkably self-righteous little speech I'd felt obliged to make, but at least they had all calmed down. Hattie Mae and Chris, if I could believe my eyes, were sitting together in front of the fire drinking tea. Teresa,

Grace, and Jake, around a small table, were sipping various liquids out of small glasses and talking, while Janet sat alone, reading. Only one electric light had been turned on, but oil lamps glowed all over the room, creating a coziness that belied the howl of the wind.

There is a kind of camaraderie, sometimes, that pulls people together in an emergency. I remembered the winter, long ago in Indiana, when a world-without-end blizzard had struck, and we were all stuck in our houses for days before they managed to get the streets plowed and the stores open. Neighbors Frank and I didn't even know stopped by to ask if we needed anything from the grocery; they had organized a flotilla of kids with sleds and were walking to the nearest open market, two miles away.

Perhaps the same spirit of "we're all in this together" had possessed the Chicago group. I hoped so. Given, however, the abrasive nature of their relationships with each other, I was far from confident.

Teresa saw me standing in the doorway and beckoned me over to join them. Jake looked me over as I sat down. "I like that sweater. You feeling better?"

"Yes, thank you. Also in a better temper, you'll be glad to know."

And that seemed to be that. Apologies were understood to have been exchanged. I sipped the gin and tonic Grace ordered for me and tried to relax.

We all winced when something struck the house with a loud crash.

"Tree limb," said Andrew, who was tending the bar. "I reckon. I can't see for certain with the shutters in place."

"How bad is it going to be, Mr. Campbell?" asked Grace.

"Bad," he said, polishing a glass. "The Met says not a hurricane, precisely, but force-eight winds, at the least, and rain enough to swamp the small boats at anchor."

"Do they say how long it will last?"

"The worst may be over by tomorrow."

He seemed calm enough, but then, as he implied, there was no point in worrying about a situation over which we had no control. He and Hester had done what they could to prepare for the storm; now we would all just have to sit it out.

Teresa spoke the question we were all thinking. "Will this house be safe?"

"Well, now, that's in the hands of God, isn't it? It's survived for two hundred years, now. Likely it'll see this storm through, as well."

I shivered. "Well, I don't mind admitting I'm scared. We don't have hurricanes in Indiana. And I worry about the search for Bob's body, too. They won't be able to get back to it until the wind and waves go down, and who knows if they'll ever find it by that time."

Andrew shook his head. "Aye, it's worrisome. I'm hoping they won't need to climb about in Fingal's Cave. The basalt is dangerous when it's wet, very slippery."

Oh, dear heaven! Now they all knew! I looked around quickly, to check reactions, but everyone was tense; I could see nothing on any face that seemed to indicate guilt. I shivered again as Hester came into the room.

"Dinner is ready, if you'd like to come through."

13

Hester, or probably Andrew, had pulled the small dining room tables together, forming one long table. It was sound psychology, I thought, meant to foster the communal warmth that was beginning to establish itself. People like to huddle together in the face of danger.

Only Janet seemed unhappy with the arrangement, seating herself at one end and establishing an invisible, but obvious, barrier. I sat next to her, but I didn't try to talk. Whatever chip she was carrying on her shoulder, she wouldn't be any more cordial if I tried to knock it off.

No, I was perfectly happy when Chris, who sat on my other side, made polite conversation.

"How is the music in your English church, Mrs. Martin?"

"Dorothy, please. And it's wonderful. My church is a cathedral, you know; Sherebury is a very old cathedral town. The church dates from shortly after the Conqueror, and a bit of the original building is still there, although most of it is late fifteenth, early sixteenth century, perpendicular style. The acoustics are incredible, and while the choir isn't in the very top rank — I mean, it isn't King's College — it's very, very good. The organist/choir master is Jeremy Sayers. I don't suppose you happen to know him?"

Chris raised his eyebrows. "I know of him, and I've heard some of his recordings. But he's marvelous! You're lucky."

I agreed. "Have you had a chance to hear any good music on this trip? I know you were traveling in Scotland for a while before you came to Iona."

He scowled. "Just Edinburgh, Glasgow, and Inverness. And they had us so tightly scheduled there was no time for side trips. We went to a couple of church services, Presbyterian mostly, but the music was mediocre. I had great hopes for Iona, because it's so old — plain song, maybe, perhaps even some ancient Celtic music, but . . ." He spread his hands and I laughed.

"No, music doesn't seem to be a principal interest here, does it? I don't suppose you got a chance to play any of the organs, either, did you?" I asked innocently.

"No." He looked at me curiously. "Am I imagining things, or have you got something up your sleeve? "

"Oh, dear, and I thought I was being so subtle! No, I just had an idea, that's all. The storm is so loud and scary, I thought maybe you would agree to play the piano for us after dinner. And maybe — well, maybe Hattie Mae could sing? She's really good."

"I know. But have you talked to her about this?"

"No, I told you I just thought of it." I ate a forkful of *boeuf bourguignon* and waited, a little anxiously, for his answer.

"Oh, well, I don't mind. I'd rather enjoy it, to tell the truth. Gospel is quite a change from the sort of thing I usually do. But you'd better check with her. She can't stand me, you know. She can't stand any of 'my kind.' "

He sounded bitter, and I couldn't leave it alone.

"Chris, shut me up if I get too personal, but do you get much of that kind of prejudice? I mean, in a profession where so many men *are* gay, I'd have thought . . ."

"You'd be surprised," he said with a brittle laugh. "Not among musicians, usually, but there are a lot of rednecks in the Midwest. And they tend to show up in churches, good Christians thinking they have a mandate from God to hate me."

"Well, to tell the truth, I'm not too sure

how I feel about homosexuality myself, but one thing I am sure about is that God never meant us to hate anybody. People's actions, maybe — but on the other hand, we were told not to judge. And I assume if you want my opinion, you'll ask. Does an ambivalent attitude offend you?"

"No. You're honest, anyway, and that's rather refreshing. It's people who are trying to save my soul, or the opposite, the ones who try to make a hero out of me because I *am* gay . . ." He cast a dark look at Teresa, across the table. "And by the way, I'm celibate. By choice."

"I didn't ask," I said hastily. "Okay, I'll sound Hattie Mae out about a concert. I think she's mellowing a little; maybe it's the storm. And surely even she, in the wake of Bob's death —"

"Are you saying that this is a memorial for Bob, this concert of yours?"

"Well, no, I didn't particularly —"

"Because if it is, count me out! I couldn't stand the guy while he was alive, and I don't intend to make pretty music for him now that he's dead!"

I waited, with a mixture of surprise and fascination, for him to go on, but he had evidently said all he intended to say, and simply sat there glaring at me.

"No, Chris, I didn't mean it that way, and there's no reason the music has to be religious, either. I just thought we needed something to cheer us up. You know, 'Eat, drink, and be merry, for tomorrow we may die.'"

It was a shame that the wind rose just then, and I had to raise my voice. The silly remark came out as a shout, and did not exactly serve to lighten the mood.

It was after dinner, however, when we were gathered in the lounge eating our blackberry crumble and drinking coffee, that I utterly shattered our desperate attempts to pretend that it was a normal evening.

I looked around for my familiar little bowl licker. He was nowhere to be seen, despite the quantity of thick, rich cream that the humans were pouring over their desserts.

"Where's Stan?" I said.

It was a casual question, to begin with, but it started a desultory search. There weren't many places to look in the lounge. He wasn't under any of the chairs, nor in either bookcase, nor in the wood box. A prickle of alarm began to rise.

"Stan's a people cat," said Teresa, her voice worried. "He ought to be here, where the people are. Where do you suppose . . . ?"

"He's a greedy wee beggar," said Andrew, who was serving the coffee. "I'd have thought he'd be after the cream. I'll check the kitchen."

He wasn't in the kitchen. He wasn't curled up on or under any of the dining room furniture. He wasn't in the office, nor in the tiny private parlor behind the office that the Campbells used as a hideaway.

The cat lovers in the group were by now thoroughly alarmed. "The bedrooms," said Chris. "Maybe he got scared of the wind and high-tailed it under one of the beds."

We searched. Even Grace and Janet, who said they hated cats, joined in. We searched every bedroom, including the ones that weren't in use. Apart from uncovering some interesting insights into our fellow guests (the extreme tidiness of Grace's room and the wild disarray of Teresa's, the stash of *Country Life* magazines that Chris kept under his bed, the bottled water in Jake's closet, and the pitiful little stack of comic books on Bob's bedside table), we were unsuccessful. No Stan.

I tried not to panic. "Cats are very good at hiding, you know. I swear, both of mine dematerialize sometimes. He's probably just upset by the storm, and found a place to sit it all out."

But Hester shook her head slowly. "He's not that way. He likes to be smack in the middle when anything interesting's going."

"And when he does hide, he has his favorite places," Andrew added. "We know them all, and we've looked. He isn't there."

"All right, then," said Jake commandingly. "When's the last time anybody saw the cat?"

There was a pause.

"He came around to see me this afternoon," I said. "He wanted to share my lunch. I finally chased him off, and I haven't seen him since."

"How do you know it was him?" demanded Janet. "There are gray tiger cats all over this island, and your cottage is a long way for him to go."

Chris, Teresa, and I looked at her pityingly.

"There's no mistaking one cat for another, if you pay attention," said Chris. "They're as different as people."

"Well, they all look alike to me," said Janet stubbornly. "Anyway, this cat, or some cat, was hanging around the garden this afternoon. I was trying to show these people the way to protect their plants from the storm. I didn't get very far, I must say, but you can't be nice to some people. And the blasted cat was getting in our way, playing with the rags

I was using to tie up the mums. I finally threw a turnip at him, and he took off down the road, toward the Abbey."

She folded her arms defiantly and stared us all down. "I didn't hit him with the turnip."

That was as close as she was going to come to an apology, and all the dirty looks in the room weren't going to make her open her mouth again.

Apparently that was the last anyone had seen of Stan; at least nobody could remember catching sight of him later in the afternoon. By about four o'clock all the guests had been helping Hester and Andrew prepare the house for the coming storm, putting up the shutters, taking in the lawn furniture. Stan hadn't been in evidence, inside or out.

We looked at each other. The wind howled. The cries of a cat could never be heard over that uproar.

Jake and Chris moved as one man. "Back door first?" asked Jake.

"It's the one he uses most," Chris agreed.

Grace caught their meaning and moved to bar their progress. "Are you out of your minds?" she demanded. "Do you intend to open that door to look for a cat? *A cat?* Do you realize you may never be able to shut it again? He'd be drowned by now, anyway! "

The men said nothing, but gently pushed past her and went down the hall.

It wasn't until they had checked the back door, wrestled it shut again with Andrew's help and started for the front, that Teresa made up her mind.

"I'm going to look for him," she announced, and headed for the front door with them.

This time Grace's wasn't the only protest. A chorus arose, my voice among them.

"Teresa, Grace has a point. He's probably right here in the house somewhere, but if not, either he's found shelter someplace, or he's already . . . anyway, there's no point in risking your life. You do realize that's what you'd be doing? If you got hit by a branch, or a roof tile, you'd —"

She turned to me, eyes blazing. "And who's to say my life's worth more than his? Most animals are a lot nicer than most people. Anyway, St. Francis is my patron saint."

"What's that got to do with it?" demanded Hattie Mae from the edge of the nervous group, but I thought I understood. If it had been one of my cats out there in that torment of wind and rain . . . but Teresa was being either more heroic or stupider than I, depending on your point of view. Stan wasn't her cat.

Jake and Chris stood by the door, unwilling to open it lest Teresa dart out. Hester and Andrew looked at each other, a succession of emotions chasing across their faces — fear and worry and exasperation and indecision. Finally, Andrew cleared his throat.

"He's our wee moggie. If anyone's daft enough to go looking for him in all this, it ought to be me." Hester, whose hands were clasped, white-knuckled, at her waist, opened her mouth, but Andrew went on. "And I'm not going, and I'm not allowing any of you out of the house. That's flat. He's a fine wee friend, and if he never comes back he'll be missed, but he's safe or he's not, and we'll have no lives risked." Andrew had already locked the back door. Now he took a key out of his pocket, turned it in the front door with a sharp little click, and stomped into the kitchen.

There's a lot to be said for Italian family influence. Teresa recognized authority when she heard it. She didn't like it, and her eyes blazed, but she went back to the lounge, indignation in every stiff line of her body, and sat as far away from Janet as she could get.

I sat next to her. She turned her head away. "It was a brave thing you tried to do," I said mildly. "I love cats, too."

"That's not the point!" she said furiously. "It's the principle —"

"Teresa, actions taken to defend a principle are dangerous. That's the sort of thing that leads to horrors like holy wars and the Inquisition. And you know perfectly well you did it out of love. Or tried to. If it was a stupid idea, at least it was nobly stupid."

"Are you calling me Don Quixote?" She was outraged.

"Of course I am. Now don't slam your fist down on that table; it's an antique, and fragile, I should think."

"You're worried about a piece of furniture when that poor cat is out there dying?"

I sighed and wished I had a drink in my hand. My patience had to work overtime to keep up with Teresa.

"My dear girl, if I thought for a moment that Stan was foolish enough to let himself get caught out in a hurricane, I'd be extremely worried about him. He's a nice, friendly cat, and I love cats, as I said. But he's also a tough, intelligent animal. I haven't the slightest doubt that he'll turn up, warm and dry, when he feels like it."

Or at least, if I had doubts, I intended to

keep them to myself. Given any encouragement at all, Teresa would bolt.

"Tell me about yourself, Teresa. You got your master's in — sociology, was it?"

"Social work," she corrected sulkily. "From Loyola."

"And what did you intend to do with it? You weren't a nun at that point."

She looked at me sharply. "How did you know that?"

"You said so. When you were arguing with Hattie Mae the other night. Or at least you implied it."

"Okay. I thought — well, anyway, no, I wasn't. I wanted to get into work with women, a shelter for battered women, something like that. And then I got to know a couple of other students, and found out they were nuns in this really liberal order. I mean, I thought nuns still wore veils and lived behind walls and all that, like when I was a kid in grade school."

All that long time ago, I thought, hiding a smile. At least ten or fifteen years. She must have gone to a very conservative school, if that was the kind of nun she knew best. Even I had known a few sisters, back in Hillsburg, and they wore blouses and skirts and seemed bound by few really archaic rules. None of them, however, had

212

prepared me for Teresa.

"So anyway, Nancy and Sue both want to be priests eventually. That's why they joined the Congregation of St. Hortense. It's really small, and liberal, like I said, and they encourage the women to seek their own destiny, and work for change. I mean, the Catholic Church is about fifteen hundred years out of date, isn't it?"

I murmured something encouraging. I wasn't sure I agreed with her, but she'd talked herself into a better mood, and I didn't want to stem the flow. Besides, I was vitally interested in her background.

"So for a while I thought about the priesthood, too, but let's face it. Nothing's going to happen in the Vatican for years and years, and I can't wait that long. So I decided to be a nun, to be in on the action, and I wangled this assignment I told you about, working with AIDS mothers and helping find homes for their babies."

"It sounds heartrending. I admire you for being able to face up to that kind of tragedy."

"It isn't as bad as you might think. They're just people; they have good days and bad days. We're not allowed to get too involved with them; they switch us around so we only work with one mother for a little while, and then somebody else takes over. I hate most rules, and it hurts, sometimes, but even I can see it's for the best. The babies — well, not all of them are HIV positive, you know. The healthy ones aren't hard to place. The sick ones — yeah, the sick ones, and the addicted ones — they break your heart."

Time to change the subject. "And how did you get to know Bob Williams?"

She looked away. "I didn't really know him very well. And what I did know I didn't like much." She studied the hands in her lap.

"My dear child," I said gently, "don't feel so guilty about it. We can't like everybody who's going to die suddenly! I should have said, how did you come into contact with him?"

"He worked with kids a lot." Her eyes were still downcast.

Find another subject. "What do you do in your time off? Any hobbies?"

She stood up, her face set and the fire back in her eyes. "I volunteer at the Humane Society. Excuse me."

She had spoken loudly enough to be heard by the whole room, even over the everlasting roar of the wind. Andrew, who was putting logs on the fire, rose to his full, imposing height, his jaw set. "I'll remind you, miss —"

I don't know for sure who would have won that contest of two formidable wills if a diversion hadn't occurred.

Stan, yawning, wandered into the lounge, stretched, and then sat looking intently at the small table where the empty dessert bowls were stacked.

14

I nobly refrained from saying "I told you so." The cat was greeted with cries of delight by everyone except Janet, who glanced at him with active dislike, but made no comment. Teresa confronted him.

"And just where have you been, cat? You've had us worried sick!"

Stan's only response was another meaningful stare at the dessert bowls. Teresa put one on the floor and poured in a little extra cream. Stan advanced and dealt with it, his rusty purr at full volume, while Teresa looked on with the fond, foolish look that only a true animal lover, or a new mother, can produce.

Well, that settled her down for the time being. That volatile personality was apt to produce more little dramas before the storm was over, but for the meantime she was occupied. That meant I could approach Hattie Mae about my concert project.

She was less difficult about it than I had expected, perhaps because I managed to hit upon a diplomatic approach. She was sitting by herself on one of the couches, eyes closed and lips moving silently as the wind increased in intensity, and I suppose I shouldn't have interrupted her prayers, but I had the feeling I could have waited all night. I plumped down beside her and her eyes opened.

"I'm sorry, Hattie Mae, but I wanted to talk to you. I've had an idea. Another way for you to praise the Lord."

I thought that was rather clever of me, actually. Hattie Mae looked a little startled, perhaps at that particular idea coming from me (whom she obviously regarded as the next thing to a heathen), but she listened, anyway.

"You see, I have the feeling that we need something to cheer us up, take our minds off — oh, everything, the storm, and Bob's tragic end, and your interrupted travel plans. I thought some entertainment might do it, and as long as we have a good piano and two fine musicians among us — what do you think?"

"With him?" She jerked her head in Chris's direction, and her lower lip began to jut out.

I chose to misunderstand. "Oh, I'm sure he isn't as good as you are. Who is? But I'd think he'd be quite competent to do backup."

I wasn't sure I had the term right, but it was the very best honey. I held my breath.

"Well . . ."

"Wonderful!" I had to shout over a sudden scream of the wind. "Why don't the two of you work out what you want to do, and—"

The crash was like the end of the world.

It took us all a shocked moment or two to collect our wits and realize what had happened, and then we moved fast.

A sizable part of a tree had broken through the house. Wall, shutters, window, all had fallen before the force of the wind-driven limb, fallen onto the chair where Teresa, with Stan on her lap, had been sitting. There was no sound from either of them.

I hope someday I will forget the nightmare struggle to get the thing off them. With the demon force of the wind coming through the broken window, the piece of tree fought us like a living thing, shards of glass cutting the men as they tried to lift it, smaller branches reaching out like arms to claw them with sharp twigs. The limb was enormously heavy, with its mass of wood and storm-drenched leaves, but the men finally managed to raise it enough that we women could drag the chair, Teresa and all, out from under it. The sight that met us was appalling.

Blood was everywhere. Teresa had been badly cut, by both the tree and the window. She had a lump on her head that was swelling rapidly; her eyes were closed.

Stan, too, was covered in blood, though whether his own or Teresa's it was impossible to say. Andrew, recklessly disregarding broken glass, lifted him away gently while the rest of us stood, shocked into immobility.

Grace was the first one to recover.

"She can't stay here. Have you a stretcher?"

Hester shook her head, her face white.

"Then blankets will have to do. She must be laid flat and carried to a safe place. Your parlor will be best; it's in the center of the house, and the upstairs rooms are out of the question; the roof might go. You, Chris, take one of the couches to the parlor. Get Jake to help you. Move out everything else if you have to. Janet, get blankets — show her where, Hester. Hattie, you and Dorothy get cold water and towels, and Hester, when you get back downstairs, we'll need antiseptic and bandages. And I'll need a lot of help carrying her."

We accepted Grace's generalship; she obviously knew what she was doing. I did take a moment, while they were moving Teresa carefully onto the blankets spread on the floor, to ask Andrew about Stan.

He shook his head. "He's breathing, but knocked out. I've put him in the kitchen, by the stove where it's warm. I don't think he's bleeding, but he'll have to fend for himself till we've the lass looked after."

"Andrew, I — maybe I have no right to butt in, but Teresa was ready, a while back, to risk her life for Stan. I think she'd want you to make sure he's okay. There are plenty of us to take care of her."

I looked at him anxiously, and after a moment he nodded his head, slowly.

"Aye, maybe you're right at that. I'll look to him, then."

Chris and Jake had made a comfortable bed in the tiny parlor. It occupied most of the room, but we managed to maneuver the makeshift stretcher in and get Teresa situated without jostling her too much. Then Hattie and I stood duty as nurses, wringing out towels in basins of cold water while Grace gingerly removed slivers of glass and tried to stanch the flow of blood.

It was a frightening business. None of the cuts looked deep, and there were no major blood vessels involved, so far as I could tell, but Teresa was so white, and there was no response from her at all. From time to time Chris leaned over to bathe the huge lump on her head.

At last Grace stopped her grisly operations.

"That's all I can do. There's more glass, but it's in pieces too tiny to get out. I'll clean her up and put on bandages, but she needs a doctor, and fast. She's lost a good deal of blood, and I don't like the look of her head. She could have a skull fracture."

"There's no doctor on Iona," said Hester soberly. "We've a visiting doctor, but her surgery is in Bunessen."

I remembered the schedule I'd seen on the village bulletin board. It seemed like a hundred years ago. Bunessen wasn't far away, only a few miles from the west side of Mull. Right now it might as well have been on the other side of the moon.

"Then we'll have to take turns watching her. I'd be happier if she'd wake up, but perhaps it's better for her that she doesn't, for a while. She's going to hurt like hell when she comes to."

So a strange sort of rhythm established itself. Grace took first watch, herself, for an hour, while the rest of us tried to rest. The lounge doors had been shut and barricaded with furniture from the parlor. There was no point in trying to repair the hole in the wall now; we could only try to keep the rain and wind from invading the rest of the house. The braver souls, Jake and Chris and Janet, went up to their rooms to try to sleep until their watch came round. The rest of us settled in odd corners wherever we could find a space.

I doubt I could have slept, even in a more comfortable spot than the small chair in front of the lounge door. As the gusts of wind came, the doors and the chair rattled and shook. Every time I opened my eyes, nervously, I checked my watch, afraid I'd oversleep for my five o'clock stint, but there was more on my mind than the duty roster.

I was afraid, of course. Afraid of the storm, afraid for Teresa, afraid for poor little Stan. Andrew had cleaned him up as best he could, and found no open wounds, but there was a nasty lump on his head, too, poor kitty, and he was still unconscious.

But worse than my concrete fears were the vague ones that kept resurfacing. Every time sleep came near, my treacherous mind replayed the tape of Bob's fall. And every time, I saw the wet rocks, and wondered why they were wet. Accident, said a panicky little voice. *Yeah, sure,* replied a cynical one. *I wish*

I could talk to Alan was my last thought before I finally did drift off into an uneasy doze.

I must have genuinely slept for an hour or two, though, because when I felt a hand on my shoulder and opened my eyes, I thought the wind sounded less fierce.

"Jake, the storm! Is it . . . ?"

"Yeah, it's maybe dying down a little. Listen, could you come? It isn't five yet, but I don't like the sound of Teresa's breathing."

I staggered to my feet and followed Jake to the parlor.

Teresa lay where we had put her, eyes still shut, but she was moving uneasily. There was a bluish look around her lips that I didn't like at all, and her breathing did indeed seem labored.

"Jake, go get Grace! I don't know which is her room, or if she went upstairs at all, but you'll have to find her. She's the only one of us who has any medical knowledge, and this looks serious."

When Jake was gone, I stood there in anxious uncertainty, trying to think what to do. Teresa was obviously in bad shape. I tried to bathe the lump on her forehead, but she turned away, fretfully, and I wanted her to move as little as possible, so I stopped.

"Teresa! Can you hear me? You must try

not to move. You're badly hurt, but you're going to be fine. Just try to lie still. You'll be fine."

I repeated the phrase almost as a prayer. She needed more help than we could give her if she was going to be fine.

She opened her eyes, startling me. They were unfocused, and one pupil seemed bigger than the other. That, I thought I remembered, was a bad sign, indicating possible brain damage.

She moaned and thrashed about feebly.

"Yes, you've been badly cut, and it must hurt terribly, but there's still glass in you, and it's better if you don't move. Can I do anything for you?"

Her lips moved in something like words. I leaned closer to her face.

"Water." At least it sounded like that. I knew better than to try to give her water, but surely there would be some ice somewhere. I didn't dare leave her to find it, though. Where on earth was Jake?

"Yes, dear, I'll get you some in a moment. I wish I could make you feel better!"

She moaned again, moved her arms, and shrieked.

"Oh, love, do try to keep still," I said in despair. "It'll be better, really."

"What's going on?"

I looked up to see Chris in the doorway. His blond hair was sticking up on one side like a sleepy child's.

"I heard a scream. What's happening?"

"Teresa's conscious, or almost, and hurting a lot. She wants some water, but I think I remember you're not supposed to give it to someone with a head injury. Can you find some cracked ice, do you think?"

"No." The faint sound came from Teresa's lips. "Not ice. Water."

Chris sighed and went in search of ice, and Grace appeared, looking twenty years older without her careful makeup and impeccable grooming.

I brought her up to date, briefly, and she gave the patient a sharp once-over.

"Yes, you're right. Definitely some injury to the brain, and she's not breathing properly. We have to get her some oxygen, and we have to get her to a doctor. Surely there's some emergency equipment somewhere on this damned island! I'll watch her while you wake the Campbells."

Chris came in then with some crushed ice in a glass, and I watched for a moment while Grace tried to give Teresa a spoonful. She turned her head away and moaned, and I went to find Hester and Andrew.

It took Andrew only a moment to grasp

the situation. "Aye, they've oxygen at the Abbey; I'll rouse them."

"And I need the front-door key."

He pointed to the dresser and didn't ask why, bless the man. I got the key and hastened back to the parlor.

"How is she?"

"No change," said Grace. "She won't take the ice."

I shook my head at that. "I guess she's still not quite with it. Oxygen's coming; Andrew's taking care of it. And I'm going down to ask David MacPherson if he can use his radio to get us some help."

"You're going out in the storm?" said Chris.

"It's not quite as bad as it was, and I have to." I looked pointedly at Teresa, quieter now, but still blue and gasping.

"I'll come with you, then."

Wordlessly we slipped down the hall, unlocked the front door, wrestled it open, and manhandled it shut again after us.

15

"Shouldn't we take Andrew's car?" Chris shouted over the wind. The storm, though possibly waning, was appalling. We were soaked with rain the minute we stepped outside the door.

"It wouldn't do us much good," I shouted back. "There'll be trees down in the road. Anyway, he'll have to try to get the car to the Abbey; oxygen tanks are heavy. But we need a flashlight."

There was no light anywhere in the world; we might have been inside a flooded, blustery cave. Living in town, one forgets the full, horrific force of the word "dark." There's always a streetlight somewhere, or headlights, or the friendly lamp in somebody's window. But Iona in the middle of a storm — I put my hand in front of my face, just to check. I actually couldn't see it.

"I've got a light, wait a minute," Chris screamed, and after a moment a strong beam showed us rain, if little else.

"Okay, then, let's go. We need to hurry as much as we can!"

We tried, but every few yards something was in the road, trees or slates or flowerpots or fence wire, and once, sickeningly, a dead sheep that we stumbled over before we saw it. Hazards were probably still flying through the air; I hoped we didn't find out for sure. The footpath would have saved time if we could have found it, but Chris's flashlight was barely enough to show us the road. So we struggled along as best we could, and I appreciated Chris's steadying arm.

All tribulations come to an end eventually. With the wind screaming in from the west, we were sheltered slightly from the worst of it once we got to the village. I had no trouble spotting David's house, and Chris hammered on the door until Fiona opened it.

"I'm sorry, Mrs. MacPherson, but we have an emergency up at the hotel. Is Mr. MacPherson awake?"

"Aye," came a deep male voice from the interior of the cottage. Fiona stood aside and gestured us in, barring the door behind us against the ever-intrusive wind.

Like the hotel's, all the windows in the MacPhersons' cottage were shuttered. Unlike the Campbells, however, David and Fiona had no electric generator, so the only light came from kerosene lamps here and there. The tiny hallway was dark, but I could see that David was fully clothed, if unshaven. Fiona, too, was dressed; either these people were *very* early risers, or they had been up all night — probably the latter, trying to protect their house and worrying about the *Iolaire*.

"We're sorry to disturb you, but I need to use your radio, Davie." Thank goodness I remembered in time that he had asked me to use his first name. This was no time to risk offense. "A woman up at the hotel was badly injured last night. A tree came through the wall, and she took a nasty blow to the head. She's just taken a turn for the worse. Is there any chance at all that you could raise a helicopter, to get her to a doctor?"

Davie considered, his face grave. This was a man accustomed to dealing with serious situations, promptly and competently.

"I can radio the Coastguard," he said at last. "They'll know what helicopters are available, and whether it's safe tae get them oot — which I doot, masel'."

"Does the doctor in Bunessen have a radio?"

"Aye."

"Then maybe you should talk to her first,

see what she recommends."

He beckoned us into the family living room. Chris stood behind me as Davie sat down at the radio on his desk.

It took him a while to get through to the doctor. Well, after all, it was still only — I looked at my watch — five in the morning. Still, a doctor ought to be used to being awakened at godforsaken hours — ah, at last!

"Ye'd best talk to her yoursel', as ye're the one who knows aboot the patient." Davie gestured me to his chair and handed me the mike.

The next few minutes were frustrating. The doctor asked questions I could barely hear, many of which I didn't know the answer to anyway. Chris and I did the best we could with a description of injuries and symptoms, and got the doctor's opinion, finally, that Teresa shouldn't be moved until she could be seen to by trained personnel. We were given instructions to carry out as best we could, including medicines to be obtained from the doctor's office — the "surgery," next to the school. The doctor told us where the surgery key was hidden and promised to be here as soon as she could arrange transport.

"Ye'll no' have the only emergency, ye

know. I'm no' saying yon lass isna bad, but there'll be mair before we've done, and me the only doctor this side the island. I'll do whit I can."

And with that we had to be content.

"I'll radio aboot yon helicopter, dinna ye worry. We'll have yon uppity doctor here soon, I promise."

I took a good deal more comfort from Davie's promises than from the doctor's.

The wind had dropped even in the little time we'd been in the cottage. It was no more now than a terrible storm, raining cats and dogs and with a wind you could stand up against. By comparison with the tempest we'd lived through, it felt like a spring drizzle.

Chris tucked my arm into his again as we walked through the stormy blackness, and kept me from falling more than once. He was silent the whole way back, but spoke as we neared the hotel. "I'll go on up to the surgery. I only hope I can find the key and the medicine. You're worn out; you go on in and get some rest."

"Thanks, Chris, I'll do that. And thanks for the moral support — as well as physically holding me up a time or two, come to think of it."

"More of a man than you might have

thought, in fact?" He laughed lightly and went on up the road, bent to the freezing wind.

I wished he wouldn't be quite so defensive. I meant him no harm. But then I entered the hotel and forgot all about him in my anxiety for Teresa.

She was better, in a way. The oxygen had improved her color, but it was also keeping her conscious, and the pain in her eyes was terrible to see. She lay very still, with Hester in watchful attendance, but she turned her head to look at me when I came in to make my report.

"Help is on the way, Teresa," I said brightly. "The doctor can't get here until the storm dies down a little more, but she agreed that the oxygen was the right thing. And she's prescribed some pain medication for you until she can get the glass out. Chris has gone to get it right now."

"Thank God," she said, and it sounded like a prayer. She closed her eyes, but a tear or two rolled out. Poor girl, she was doing her best, but how she must hurt!

I spoke a quiet word or two to Hester about dosage and general instructions. "There's not much we can do, really, until the doctor gets here. She said Teresa's not to be moved. Oh, and be sure she isn't given water, only ice. Water might make her sick. It'll be a while before we have help, but the storm's really waning, I think."

"Yes. God be thanked. Get you up to bed, now; you've done all you can and more than was to be expected, and there'll be enough to do when you wake."

It was excellent advice. I dragged myself up the stairs, stripped off my wet clothes, and fell on the bed; no sound of wind or rain disturbed me for hours.

It was almost noon when I woke, and then only with reluctance. I heaved myself off the bed and went to the window. The struggle with the shutters cost me a thumbnail, but when I finally got them open, the daylight was a blessing. The sky was still filled with clouds, but only a soft rain was falling. The wind was blowing fiercely, but no longer like all the forces of hell unleashed. I echoed Hester's sentiment: God be thanked.

The devastation, though, was terrible to behold. Hester's beautiful flowers were gone, as if they'd never existed, and her vegetable garden was a mass of mud. And that was the least of it. The garden shed was a flattened mess of wreckage. Slates littered what was left of the grass, probably slates from the roof of the hotel. I wondered how much roof was left. I turned away from the window, glanced at my ceiling, and saw a spreading stain of dampness that, as I watched, concentrated itself and began to drip steadily onto the bed.

Time to stop mourning and start moving. I wrestled the bed away from the wall, but there was nothing in the room to put under the drip. I draped a bathrobe around my underwear, wishing passionately that I had time for a bath, and dragged my still weary body downstairs.

"Did you sleep?" asked Hester, in the kitchen, looking as though she hadn't.

"Yes, thank you. I need a saucepan, or something. My ceiling's sprung a leak."

"They all have." She sounded ready to cry. "There's not a pot, nor a pail, nor a basin in the house not being used to catch water. I'll do you some lunch presently, though how I'm to cook with no pots . . ." She threw up her hands in despair and I changed the subject.

"How's Teresa?"

"Much the same. She had a wee sleep after Mr. Olafson brought the medicine, but she's not good."

"I'll go see her in a minute. What about Stan?"

Hester smiled, faintly. "Active and complaining. He's not badly hurt. He ate his breakfast and wanted more, cheeky little beggar. He's off sleeping, someplace."

"Well, that's good news, anyway. I'll pet him if I see him. And Hester, don't worry about feeding us. Cold cuts will be fine. You look as though you're about to collapse any minute."

"Oh, I'll manage. There's food enough and to spare ready in the freezer, if I can think how to heat it." She managed a rueful smile.

"I'll get out of your way, then. Do let me know, though, if there's any way I can help." I removed myself and went into the parlor.

Teresa had dropped into a light sleep. Grace put a finger to her lips when she saw me, and I beckoned her out into the hall.

"How is she?"

"Restless, and raving a bit. It's the medicine, I suppose. I hope. She isn't in quite so much pain, I think, but she keeps asking for water, and won't take the ice I try to give her. Do you have any idea when the doctor will get here?"

"No, but soon, I should think. The wind's dying down by the minute. She did say, the doctor, I mean, that there'd be other injuries she might have to deal with first. A storm like that — and there's no other doctor on the whole west side of Mull."

"Yes, well, we're not talking about a population of millions, are we? She's needed here, now."

Privately, I agreed with her, but a year of living in the UK had taught me a certain amount of patience.

"This is a pretty remote place, don't forget. And the pace of life is different here."

"I wonder what the pace of death is," said Grace sourly.

I noticed the circles under her beautiful eyes. She needed to be relieved. "Have you been up with her this whole time?"

"Since Jake woke me, yes. Someone with a modicum of medical knowledge had to be with her."

I was diverted from my purpose. "I've been meaning to ask you, Grace, how is it you know so much about first aid? Did you train as a nurse?"

"No." Her tone implied what a ridiculous question it was. "You know I work with the homeless. They have so many medical problems, any day can be an emergency at any meal center. I took a special course at Cook County."

Her tone was both patronizing and dismissive, but my respect for her went up a notch. Cook County Hospital, in one of Chicago's worst neighborhoods, isn't a place for the faint of heart.

But this wasn't the time to gush over Grace. I simply said, "I see. That explains it. Now, I'm going to take a bath and then relieve you. I've had some sleep; you haven't, or not enough. I'll be back in fifteen minutes."

A sound from Teresa sent Grace back into the parlor before she could argue with me, as she was certainly about to do. I didn't care. I was going to take over from her, and that was that. I had my own reasons for wanting to sit with Teresa.

It took me a little more time than I'd given myself, what with picking up my soggy clothes from the corner where I'd heedlessly dropped them hours before, and mopping the floor. I piled up some towels under the drip, got downstairs in reasonably good time, clean and clothed, and managed to remove Grace from her duty with no more of a fight than I had anticipated.

"I know where you are if I need you. And I promise to get you right away if the doctor comes. Go!"

Still grumbling, she went, and I settled down to listen very carefully to anything Teresa might say.

She was still asleep, and seemed to be resting fairly comfortably, when Hester poked her head in the door.

"Lunch, such as it is, is served," she whispered. "Soup and sandwiches. Shall I bring you a tray?"

"Just sandwiches, thank you. Teresa might smell the soup and want some, and she's not supposed to have anything to eat for a while. Have you had any word about when the doctor is supposed to get here?"

"Yes, Davie MacPherson talked just now to Andrew. In an hour or two, he says."

She hurried away, and I breathed a great sigh of relief. In an hour or two Teresa would be taken off our hands, as a responsibility, at any rate, even if she had to stay where she was. Myself, I hoped she could be transported to Mull or even Oban.

The farther away the better, in fact, because I was beginning to be very worried about Teresa's concern over water.

She wouldn't take ice when it was offered to her. Evidently she wasn't thirsty.

Why, then, did she keep mentioning water?

Could it possibly be that she, too, was wondering where the water in Fingal's Cave had come from? Had her mind, in trauma, wandered back to another traumatic moment? She hadn't seen Bob fall, but she had been with him on Staffa. Could she have seen him go into the cave, maybe a cave she'd just left? Suppose she'd been up to the top of the path and noticed it was perfectly dry? And then, when I'd said the rocks were wet . . .

But I hadn't said they were wet. That was the one piece of information I'd kept to myself, except for telling the police. So had she seen the rocks? How else would she know?

Either they'd been wet when she was in there, and she'd thought of the significance only when Andrew mentioned the danger, or else she herself . . .

Now stop it! my inner censor commanded. *Not Teresa!*

But then, I didn't want it to be any of them. I sighed. I was building an awful lot of theory on a very little evidence. Maybe Teresa just hated ice.

She stirred again, and again said, "Water . . ."

I stood eagerly and went over to her. "What is it, Teresa? Are you thirsty? They've told you, haven't they, that you can't have water, only cracked ice?"

She looked at me without comprehension, muttered something, and closed her eyes. I looked at her fingernails; they were taking on a bluish hue again. She wasn't getting any better, that was for sure. I abandoned speculation and concentrated on looking after my patient.

16

Hester came and went, bringing me sandwiches and removing the plate, and after several eternities the doctor arrived. The wind had died down enough that I could hear the beat of the helicopter blades as the machine landed, and then it was only a few minutes before the doctor strode into the parlor, bag in hand, looking tired but in control. She was older than I'd imagined, with short gray hair and a bluff, no-nonsense manner. She was accompanied by the paramedics from the helicopter.

The examination took only a few minutes, while Teresa, half conscious, twisted and moaned. Then the doctor gave her a shot of something that calmed her down, and rose.

"Well, she'll need to go to hospital, but she canna be transported with all yon glass in her. I'll have to get as much of it oot as I can, masel'. I'll need a long, clean table, and clean sheets." She looked at Hester, who was hovering anxiously.

"The kitchen table's six feet long, if that'll do."

"Aye. Noo, are ye ready to lift her?" She took one corner of the blanket, the paramedics the others, and transferred Teresa, as gently as possible, to the stretcher. Her blood had soaked through the blankets to Hester's couch, I noticed irrelevantly. It was never going to be the same again.

Everyone was banished from the kitchen while the grisly procedure was going on. I was just as glad. I don't cope well with blood, myself, and I can't stand to see anyone suffer. I drifted to the hall and stood, irresolute. I should wake Grace, as I'd promised, but she wasn't needed right now, and the poor woman had to have some sleep.

Stan decided the matter for me. Thrown out of the kitchen with the rest of us, he walked across the hall, staggering a little, and headed for his favorite spot by the fire in the lounge. I followed, if only to see how he was doing.

While I had slept, others had been at work. The lounge was not a pleasant place this afternoon, but one could sit there, at least. The ruined furniture and sopping rugs had been removed, with what wearisome effort I could only imagine. There are few things as heavy and awkward as a large, wet rug. The hole in the wall was patched with plywood, ugly and impermanent, but at least offering some protection from the still churlish weather. A few dining room chairs sat around, pretending to be comfortable armchairs.

Janet was the sole occupant of the room; she sat on the one couch that had apparently escaped the furies of the storm. Stan, of course, made straight for it and jumped up beside her. I scooped him up before he could make it to her lap. Like every cat I have ever known, Stan had an unerring instinct for the people who didn't like him, and loved to torment them with his demanding presence. I settled him by my side, petted him until I thought he would stay there, and then peered over to look at what Janet was reading — or pretending to read. She had been turning the pages very fast and, apparently, at random. It didn't surprise me that it was a gardening book.

"That's a beautiful book," I said with little hope of a response.

"Do you want it? I'm tired of reading." She tossed the heavy book onto the cushion between us and woke Stan, but only momentarily, thank goodness.

"Not really. I want to talk. Do you mind? I'd like to take my mind off the storm, and the damage, and especially Teresa, poor dear."

Janet shrugged.

I picked up the gardening book. "Do you suppose I could learn anything from this?" I persisted. "I'm a hopeless gardener, but I do love flowers. I understand you're quite a gardener."

"It's my life."

"Oh, you're a professional landscape gardener, then? "

"Of course, what did you think?" And she turned her back to me and stared at a window. She didn't see much; the shutters were still up.

I'm easily cowed by rudeness, but I was determined to get Janet to talk. So I sat and looked at the back of her neck until, sure enough, she started to squirm, and turned to glare at me.

I smiled back as sweetly as I could manage. "I do wish you'd tell me about your gardening. I admire people who can make things grow, but I've never had a green thumb."

That got through to her. She snorted. "Green thumb, hah! Gardening's nothing more than a few ideas and a lot of back-breaking work. People talk as if there's something magical about it."

"For me there is," I persisted. "I used to work very hard, but my seeds wouldn't come up, or they'd die, or not bloom, or get eaten by bugs or choked by weeds. I finally decided it takes talent, and hired a gardener."

"It takes knowing what you're doing, that's all. You have to know your soil, and your climate, and where the sun's going to be, and what plants do well together. Now take that old idea about planting roses and garlic together." She was well launched, and for half an hour I was treated to a lecture on horticulture. She obviously knew what she was talking about, and I learned some things, but I wanted to know more about Janet, herself.

"Tell me," I broke in when she paused for breath, "about your church gardens. I understand that's why you won this trip, your church landscaping?"

She gave a scornful little wave, and her lined, weathered gardener's face fell into a frown. "Child's play, volunteer work. I had to plant things the church volunteers could take care of, and most of them don't know one end of a spade from the other. Roses. Petunias. Marigolds. And lots of evergreens that only need cutting back to look perfect, but do the idiots do it? Oh, no, come back to me in a year or two and whine about how the greenery is taking over, and what should they do? I swear, most of them never heard of pruning shears. The worst of them all was that Bob, I tell you."

"You mean Bob? The Bob who —"

"And good riddance, I say. He was a world-class twit. What *he* wanted was a garden his sweet little darlings could take care of. Now have you ever known a kid you could get to put in a day's work in the hot sun? Much less when they've got a spineless fool like Bob Williams in charge of them. So his flowers would die, and then he'd come back and blame me, and tell me I had to plant something easier for them, and teach them what to do with it. I finally told him nobody paid me for all this, and nobody *could* pay me enough to baby-sit his little juvenile delinquents, and he should just put down green concrete and with any luck the kids would get buried under it. He went sniveling to his bishop, and I thought I never would hear the end of it. Oh, he's no loss to the world, I can tell you!"

I heard a cough behind us, and turned. Andrew was standing there holding a kerosene lamp and looking shocked.

"And what's the matter with *you?*" Janet demanded.

"Nothing at all, Miss Douglas," he said stiffly. Plainly, he found Janet's attitude toward the dead unseemly, but couldn't say so to a guest. "I've come to tend to the lamps. If you'll excuse me." He picked up another one and strode out of the room.

"Hmph! Doesn't want to use his precious electricity, I suppose," Janet muttered. "It's true what they say about the Scotch. Cheapskates, every one of them."

"It's 'Scots,' not 'Scotch,'" I said coldly. "Scotch is the drink, but over here they just call it whiskey, anyway. If you're going to be in the country, you might as well get the language right. It's only courteous."

Janet turned on me furiously. "And why should I care about being courteous to *them?* What have they ever done for me, that I should be nice to *them?*"

I moved away an inch or two, and Stan, sensing the atmosphere, prudently took off. "I see," I said slowly. "You have a personal vendetta, don't you?"

Her face closed up. "I don't know what you mean," she said in a flat voice.

"Oh, come now. You've been rude and uncooperative ever since you came here, and you obviously hate Scotland and all its works with a genuine passion. Why would you have come on the trip, if you didn't have something to prove? It's a family matter, I suppose. With a name like Douglas, you probably have Scottish origins."

I stopped. Her face had turned blotchy, a dull brick red alternating with pasty white. I seemed to have touched a raw nerve.

"And if I do, what business is it of yours?"

"None."

I let it lie there, and she broke the silence, as I thought she would.

"It was my father," she began, in an odd, flat tone of voice. "He came from these parts. Or at least that's what he told my mother. They met during the war. She was from the Lowlands, a farm outside a little village called Dalmellington, but she went to Glasgow to do war work when all the men were called up. There was constant naval traffic in and out of Glasgow, because of the shipyards."

I nodded. I knew very little about the impact of World War II on Scotland, but I did know that Glasgow had been a world center of shipbuilding.

"He was in the navy, and a good-looking louse, from what my mother said. They met at a dance, and she was swept right off her feet. She used to talk about him sometimes, when she was drunk."

This story was not going to have a happy ending.

"It lasted a couple of weeks, I guess. Then he was shipping out, and he asked her to marry him, but they couldn't get a license in time. If he ever intended to.

"When she found out I was on the way, she tried to get hold of him, but it turned out he wasn't on the ship he had told her he'd be on. Probably nothing he'd told her was the truth, except he was a sailor, for sure. She loved his uniform."

Janet laughed, a bitter sound with no mirth in it. "I don't remember much about the war, of course. I was too little. Mother had to take me back home to the farm, but her parents were hard people, and as soon as the war was over she took me to America. Some people from the village kirk had relatives in Chicago who were willing to sponsor us, and her parents scraped together the fare somehow.

"I do remember the trip. I was sick the whole time, and so was my mother. Then we had to get on a train to get to Chicago, and it was crowded — oh, I just remember it was all awful, and I cried and cried. I was only five, but I remember that.

"The rest is the usual story. Mother found work, but there weren't good day care centers then, so if I was sick and couldn't go to school, she'd have to stay home. One job after another lost, no money — you've heard it all before. It happened to thousands of gullible girls. She was thirty-two when she died and I had to go to an orphanage. But eventually I got an education and found a place to live where I could have a little garden — and that's my life story. Dull, isn't it?"

Her voice dared me to express any sympathy, so I kept my face as neutral as I could. "So you've come to Iona to try to find your father? He'd be a very old man now, wouldn't he?"

"Seventy-five, eighty. If he's still alive. I didn't think I'd find him actually on Iona. I knew it was a very small island. But I thought there might be relatives, someone who could put me on the track. I'd like to meet someone related to him, so I could tell them to their face what a gold-plated son of a bitch they had in their family."

"And were you successful?" I was sure I knew the answer.

"His name was MacLean. Do you have any idea how many MacLeans there are in the Edinburgh phone book? Or Glasgow? It was a stupid idea from the start. I've done a little scouting around here, but no one remembers a Bruce MacLean who went to war in 1942. That was a lie, like everything else. Or else *they're* lying. I wouldn't put it past them. Sneaky, as well as stingy."

So that explained her fight with the farmer. "Janet," I said cautiously, "your mother was a Scot, too. How can you hate the Scots so much, when it's your heritage on both sides?"

"That was what that wimp Bob tried to tell me, too. Crap about loving your neighbor, and forgiveness, and that gentle Jesus meek and mild line. Well, he's dead, so I don't have to hear it from him anymore, and I don't have to hear it from you either, thank you very much." She stalked out of the room, and after a moment I rose, wearily. I had been forcibly reminded of why I preferred the solitude of my cottage.

And, although heaven only knew what my poor little domain must look like after the storm, it was time I headed back to it. I did open the kitchen door a crack to see how Teresa was doing, and saw the doctor putting away her instruments. Teresa lay very still and white on the table.

"Is she — ?" I was afraid to finish the question.

"She's alive," said the doctor brusquely. "There's pressure on the brain; she could go either way. We're off to hospital in Oban." She turned to the paramedics. "Back on the stretcher," she barked.

They went off with their burden. Several

of us watched out the front door as the men picked a careful path up the road, between the downed trees and the deep puddles. It wasn't an easy job, and we were all relieved when they got her into the helicopter. I breathed a quick prayer for her and went back inside.

Grace was in the hall.

"Did you get some rest?"

"A little. It doesn't matter. How is Teresa?"

I gave her the doctor's brief report. "It sounds pretty iffy, but at least she's in good hands now. I don't know what this will do to your travel plans —"

"We can't leave till the ferry's running, can we? I asked Mr. Campbell. He said the problem is with the boat's computer, and the part to repair it has to come from Glasgow, so . . ."

"You seem to be taking it very philosophically." I looked at her curiously.

"Dorothy, as I've tried to tell the others, I learned long ago that there is very little point in butting one's head against a stone wall. The wall does not yield, and the head suffers. When I can do something about a difficult situation, I act. When I cannot, I don't waste time fretting about it." She nodded her head sharply by way of farewell, and left.

I gathered up the few belongings I had brought with me and slipped out the door. I could pay my bill later. Just now I needed some peace.

17

My sense of unease drove me as far as the jetty, where, suddenly, I could go no farther. I sat, wet, cold, and miserable, gazing across the Sound.

Waves rose and crashed, their white tops whipped off by the wind. Swells driven by titanic forces deep at sea made the water into a living thing, roiling, writhing, demonic in its power and terror. I shivered. What it must be for any lost soul in a boat . . . or for Bob . . .

No, I didn't want to think about Bob, about his body, tossed and battered by the waves, cold . . .

Romantic nonsense! Bob was neither cold nor wet. Wherever he was, whatever his state, he was undeniably beyond mortal sensation. It was I who sat foolishly shivering in the rain. I willed myself to my feet, picked up my suitcase, and made my way through the ruins of gardens and roofs spread over the village street.

Dove Cottage looked, superficially, as if it had survived the storm reasonably well. The window boxes with their bright geraniums were gone, vanished, as if they had never existed, but the roof was intact and the windows, miraculously, had survived. It was cold and dark inside. The radiators were electric, but surely there was something to burn in the front-room fireplace, and I vaguely remembered seeing at least one oil lamp somewhere. I dragged myself to the kitchen, trying to think what to do. The lamp, fuel, matches, try to remember how to light it . . .

My energy lasted long enough to make light, and then sheer inertia took over. I abandoned the search for firewood. I left my suitcase where I had dropped it. I couldn't even find the strength to change into warm, dry clothes. There was an afghan draped invitingly across the back of the couch; wrapping it around me, I sat.

The lamp shed a warm glow. I only wished I felt as cozy as the room looked. I had reached that extremity of weariness — mental, physical, and emotional — that frays the nerves to their breaking point. I wasn't sleepy; I'd just had a nap. I was used up, done.

You're going to catch pneumonia if you sit there all wet, said my sensible voice.

I ignored it. Pneumonia might be a boon.

I could go to a warm bed in a warm hospital, where people would look after me. No one would be drowning around me, and there would be no hurricanes, no emotional scenes . . .

I had settled myself into a thoroughly maudlin mood when I heard a knock at the door. I considered ignoring it, but I was obviously at home. People may leave the house with the electric lights still on, but no one with sense goes off and leaves a kerosene lamp burning in an empty house.

I went to the door, muttering under my breath several expressions Hattie Mae would have disapproved of.

Of course I was ashamed of myself the minute I opened the door, for there stood Hester Campbell, dripping wet, and carrying two large plastic bags.

"Goodness, come in! I'm sorry it's so cold in here; I haven't gotten around to finding anything to burn. What in heaven's name brought you out?"

She headed for the kitchen and put down her parcels.

"You. When I realized you'd gone without telling us."

"Oh. I'm sorry about that, but I did intend to come up tomorrow and pay my bill. I just —"

Hester laughed, a little hysterically, I thought. "Och, it's not the bill we'd be worrying about! And I do understand why you came away. To tell the truth, I wish I could do the same. No, we just — Andrew and I — we didn't know how you'd manage down here alone, with no electricity. So I brought you some food you can eat cold if needs must, and some charcoal you can burn for warmth, and candles. But there's a wee camp stove here, I think, for heating the food. And did you know your water heater runs on Calor gas, like ours? Here, let me show you."

She bustled about and in ten minutes had the water heating for a good bath, a small charcoal fire burning in the grate, and the kerosene stove dusted, filled, and ready to light. I followed humbly in her wake, holding a candle, accepting instructions, handing her matches.

"There now! That's you settled! I'll just be off; Andrew's waiting with the car. He got as far as the jetty, but the road is too badly littered after that."

I finally found my voice. "Wait. Hester — how can I thank you? I've been such a nuisance —"

"Nonsense. If we can't help one another in an emergency, what were we put here for?

You'll come up if you need anything."

With that clear command, she was off, leaning into the wind, her hair blowing out from under her scarf, and I was shaken out of my lethargy, feeling like a particularly low variety of worm.

It wasn't surprising that Hester knew the accoutrements of my cottage better than I did. Many parts of the British Isles are still places where neighbors know each other, visit each other, help each other. No, it was that matter of helping that stuck in my throat.

"If we can't help one another . . ." And I'd deserted the hotel the moment I could get out of it.

It wasn't quite that easy, was it? There were things I still had to do. I unpacked, took a bath that was at least tepid, and put on the warmest clothes I had, long underwear and all. There was a great deal of cleaning to do up at the hotel, and I ought to help.

It's annoying, when you've gone all high-minded and made up your mind to do a good deed, to be thwarted before you've even begun. When I went downstairs, I looked out the window and realized no more cleaning was going to be done today, at least not outside. The rain was worse again, coming down in torrents. Although the wind had subsided still more, nobody could get any work done in this. There would come a time for me to be of use, but evidently it wasn't now.

Part of me was immensely relieved. I was so utterly, world-without-end weary. I sat down on the couch, in front of the small but warming fire, pulled the afghan over my lap, and felt how wonderful it was to do nothing but sit.

But the other part of me, the part that inhabited most of my being when I wasn't feeling my age so devastatingly, wanted to be up and doing. I remembered a small great-nephew of mine who had once come upon his mother and me when we were sitting on her California patio, luxuriating in the sunshine and stillness. "What are you doing?" he asked.

"Nothing," was my reply. "Just enjoying doing nothing."

He considered for a moment. "But isn't that awfully boring?"

He was right. It was.

And then there was the other, more insidious scourge of idleness. For when you're busy, when you're fully occupied with busyness, you can put off unpleasant thoughts for a long time. When you're doing nothing, thoughts come thick and fast, and it's hard to beat them off.

There were many thoughts I didn't want to think, and they were all centered around Bob Williams, a young man I had never really known and had certainly never liked. But he was dead, and I wanted, needed, to know why.

I also wanted to know what Teresa Colapietro meant when, in her delirium, she kept repeating the word "water."

Finally, I wanted to know why Teresa was so much worse in the middle of the night than she had seemed just after the blow to her head.

Because, no matter how hard I tried to shut out the picture, I kept coming back to that fall of Bob's, that horrific, slow-motion fall, and the water-glazed rocks where no water should be. And I knew the nightmare would haunt me until I knew for certain whether or not he had been murdered.

I had to accept the fact that no one was going to help me with this. With no telephone, possibly for several more days, I couldn't call Alan. The local police didn't believe a word of what I'd tried to tell them, and were, in any case, unavailable except for a dire emergency.

No, if anyone was going to do anything

about the situation, it would have to be me.

It was perhaps just as well, I thought grimly as I pulled the afghan a little closer, that I was stuck in this cottage with nothing to do but think. A great deal of thinking needed to be done, and the result of it had better be cogent and correct.

Very well. The time had come to make the list I'd never gotten around to. The only paper in the house, as far as I knew, was the telephone pad, so I struggled out of my woolly cocoon, got the pad from the kitchen and a pen from my purse, and began, snuggled up again, to think in earnest.

Means, motive, opportunity. The classic three points of investigation. I'd already decided that everyone had, or could have had, both the means — a bottle or two of water — and the opportunity. Bottled water was ubiquitous, and anyone could have managed to be in the cave alone for a few seconds.

The risk, though! Not to the murderer, really; he — or she, there was no reason it couldn't have been a woman — could, with clever use of his or her body, have shielded the critical actions from anyone just entering the cave. Or if he — the single pronoun was easier — had been observed, he could have exclaimed over his carelessness, warned everyone, and sat down later to figure out a different method.

No, it was the sheer disregard for anyone else's safety that took my breath away. What if someone else had stepped on those deadly, wet rocks, someone who had no idea of the danger? Anyone could have died that day.

Which brought up a point. Was Bob the intended victim, or simply an unfortunate bystander?

That, I decided, was a byway I didn't intend to explore at the moment. The task was going to be hard enough without bringing in impossible complications. If I had to figure out which of six people had reason to murder any one of the other six, I had a problem which, in its sheer mathematical proportions, was to all intents and purposes unsolvable.

No, stick to what happened. Bob died. Any one of his traveling companions could have murdered him. So I was, once more, down to what was traditionally the least important of the three big questions, but was in this case the only definitive one: Who had a motive to kill him?

Although my poking around of the last few days — it didn't deserve to be called an investigation — had been inefficient in the extreme, I had, in fact, gleaned a few facts about a few people. I began the list-making.

After a good deal of memory-searching and head-scratching, the first small page of the pad read:

Hattie Mae

Disliked Bob. Thought he was ineffective as a youth leader, and "had a bad feeling" about him. Said the kids laughed about him behind his back, and implied he was, simply by his naivete, encouraging the kids' use of drugs. The mother of teenagers; feels passionately about drug influence.

Was there a motive for murder there? Just possibly, I supposed, if she felt that Bob had directly threatened her own two boys. The lioness protecting her cubs, et cetera. But there was absolutely no indication that any such threat had existed, or even that Hattie Mae thought it had, which was the point. I sighed, flipped to the next page of the pad, and adjusted the wick of the lamp so it burned a little more brightly. I wished I could likewise adjust my mind.

Grace

The only things she's said about Bob are

positive, except that she called him a young twit, or something like that. But she's an odd sort of woman. Super efficient, but very cold. Remember, "When something can be done about a problem, I act." Or words to that effect. She, of all the group, has the personality to commit a cool, impersonal murder.

Which, however, did not constitute a motive, I scolded myself. I certainly wasn't accomplishing much, and besides, the room felt chilly and I was getting hungry. Maybe if I fed my stomach, my brain would operate a trifle better.

Hester had brought me, among other things, a large jar full of potato soup. Surely I had once known how to light a camp stove?

It took me a while to remember how to pump the thing up, but once I got it going, it heated the soup in only a few minutes, and a large bowlful not only warmed me through, it had a positive influence on my mood, as well. There is something homey and solid and genuine about potato soup. When I had finished, I felt once more in possession of my right mind and a certain amount of my self confidence.

I went back to my list, promising myself some blackberry crumble when I was finished, accompanied by, for once, all the cream I wanted. A few more coals and some earnest blowing brought my fire back to life, and I settled myself, well wrapped in the afghan, to productive thought.

Chris

Chris didn't like Bob. No reason given, but Chris is a quiet sort who doesn't talk about his feelings much. He's also gentle, more interested in his music than anything else, I think. Remember his plaintive cry when he realized he was marooned on Iona: "Never see my church again, the choir, the organ . . ." Somehow I can't see him as a murderer.

But if he were to kill someone, I mused, he'd probably do it in just such an indirect, chancy way. And that was pure speculation, and utterly irrelevant. I sighed again.

Janet

Now that's a murderous personality if ever there was one. Janet's mad at the world, for good reason, perhaps. It has treated her rather shabbily. And she disliked Bob with a passion, because he had interfered with the one love of her life, her gardening. But I can't make it seem like a motive for murder. She's been preoccupied, anyway, with her search for family in Scotland.

Teresa

Another hothead. Teresa's temper is all Italian, and it doesn't seem that being a nun has modified her basically ballistic approach to life. But she's not the Borgia type, to plan and scheme against an enemy. If she's mad at you, she tells you about it now, in no uncertain terms. She could probably flatten somebody, if she got mad enough. I wouldn't be at all surprised to learn she's good at karate. But I can't imagine her doing murder. She has an active conscience, for all her fire.

And besides, I thought, shifting a little, if there was anything in my theory that Teresa was — well, somehow damaged a little further during one of those long watches of the night, then she was out of the picture as first murderer. The only motive for hurting her would involve something she knew, something the murderer couldn't afford to have get around.

Which left me with:

Jake

A nice, warm man who's had a tragic life. He'd already lost his wife and daughter when his grandson, the light of his life, committed suicide because he had the AIDS virus. The poor man's an atheist now, or says he is.

I pondered this. That could, I supposed, mean Jake didn't subscribe to the same moral code he used to. I wished, I thought fretfully, that I had any idea how Aaron had been infected. He was involved in sports, had played against some of the teams that Bob coached. I wondered if Jake had ever asked Bob; he might have seen some interaction —

The idea hit me with almost physical force; I think I actually reeled back a little. Could it have been Bob himself? All those kids he worked with, such long hours — what if he were a child molester?

Once the idea presented itself, I wondered why it hadn't been obvious before. The room seemed very cold suddenly. I wrapped the afghan around me more tightly. Perhaps it was time for a cup of coffee, if I could figure out how to make coffee without an electric coffeemaker. How spoiled I was! I began to unwind myself from the afghan.

You're delaying it. You're afraid to face it. Coward!

I put some more charcoal on the fire, quite unnecessarily, and sat back down, pad in hand.

What if Jake had found out, somehow, that Bob was a pedophile? I don't think he could have suspected before they all came on this trip. But suppose something had happened to make him suspicious of Bob. And then suppose someone had told him, when he first arrived on the island, about the rocks on Staffa being dangerous when they were wet.

No, that wouldn't work. Suspicion wouldn't have been enough. But certainty, now. If he *knew* Bob was the one who had ruined his life . . .

Would he have risked the lives of other people, though? Anyone who had happened into the cave before Bob did?

Or — it could have been another way. Suppose he sought Bob out, on Staffa, and they went into the cave together. They could have had an argument, or Jake could have accused Bob, and Bob might have admitted something — enough. Then could Jake have poured out the water and — just left?

I stopped writing. What I was picturing was horribly plausible. I could see him doing it, pouring water on the rocks like — like a libation to the ancient gods. And leaving matters, in a way, up to them. Bob might fall or he might not. If he did — I could see Jake shrugging his shoulders. In the hands of the gods. In the hands, maybe, of the Yahweh he said he didn't believe in, but who was reputed to exact swift and terrible vengeance.

The room wasn't really cold. It was cozy and warm. The lamplight was just as soft and golden, the couch just as comfortable. Then why was I so cold and miserable?

I didn't want my dessert, after all.

18

The night passed, as even the worst nights do. Untwisting the bedclothes once again, at three in the morning, I was aware that the rain had stopped, and resented the fact; its soothing sound had helped lull me to sleep for brief periods.

But morning came, eventually, a gray, cheerless morning that was only slightly less gloomy than the darkness of night. If it wasn't raining, it might at any moment. I got up because there seemed to be no point in staying in a bed that had offered no rest, and struggled with lighting the camp stove and making coffee because I hoped that acting normal might make me feel normal. There was no way to make toast, short of holding it on a fork over the gas flame. That might once, at a campground, in another lifetime, have seemed like fun. It didn't now. I ate something cold without noticing what it was, made my bed, tidied up the cottage. Act normal.

There is a merciful numbness that takes possession of us in times of great pain. I had experienced it when my beloved Frank had died. Suddenly my world was shattered, my whole life was without shape or meaning, and yet I kept on, writing the thank-you notes that had to be written, buying groceries, preparing meals for myself, going on automatic pilot until the numbness wore off and the pain took over, agonizing, but a little easier to bear because I had already established new habits.

I knew, as a kind of academic abstraction, that the dazed apathy I was feeling now would wear off soon. Facts, horrid, ugly facts would batter again at the now-closed door of my mind, clamoring for admission, for action. Meanwhile, what I felt (I decided as I sat and sipped coffee and coolly considered the question) was, astonishingly, a kind of peace.

For I had finally admitted, and accepted, what I had at some level known for some time. That, my detached mind informed me, was what I had been running away from for the past several days. Not from a group of people who were no worse than any other people anywhere, but from the certain, if unconscious, conviction that Bob had been murdered. Coldly, deliberately, with malice aforethought — and, I was now dreadfully afraid, by someone I liked a lot.

The coffee tasted awful. The pain was coming closer. It was lurking, just around the corner. It was — here.

"No!" I wailed aloud. "Not Jake — no!"

My anguished cry seemed to echo. It took me a moment to recognize the sound that persisted, and when I did I bounded up from the table to open the back door.

"Stan! Of all the wonderful — come in! Come here!"

Stan was a patient, good-natured cat. He allowed himself to be scooped up, and lay quietly purring in my arms while I sat and wept into his soft, stripy gray fur. Only when I began to sniffle and reach for a tissue did he wriggle his eagerness to be put down.

"Yes, all right. You want some ham, don't you? Or at least that's all I have to offer you. And you can have as much as you want, as a reward for turning up when I needed you."

He had restored my balance. I chopped ham for him, and poured him a little cream for dessert, and thought, with infinite sorrow, about what to do.

I wanted sleep quite desperately, but I knew it wouldn't come. The peace of a deduction reached, a dreadful idea accepted, had been a transient illusion. There was no real peace for me with so many questions left unanswered. I was sure I was right, but I hadn't the slightest iota of proof. I wanted to know what had happened between Bob and Jake to bring matters to their appalling conclusion. I wanted to know if the others had any suspicions. Especially, I wanted to know about Jake and Teresa.

She had been in his care, with everyone else asleep or at least elsewhere, when she'd taken a turn for the worse. And she had kept talking about water. That must have terrified Jake. Would he — could he — I didn't want to think so, but then I didn't want to think he had killed Bob, either.

He was such a decent man, such a warm human being! I pressed my head between my hands, hard. Was I making this whole thing up?

No. I wished I were, but no, it was real enough, and horrible enough. And what, to get back to where I started, was I to do about it?

I couldn't call the police with no telephone. Or at least, I realized suddenly, I could, if I were willing to broadcast my whole story over David MacPherson's radio. Not the most private of communications, was it? It was my legal duty to communicate with the police, but I could be jeopardizing myself or others if Jake somehow got wind of it.

Furthermore, the police had shown me what they thought of my ideas. With no clear evidence, they would do nothing.

"So there's no point, is there?" I addressed Stan, who blinked and continued to lick cream from his whiskers.

If only I could talk to Alan! He'd listen to me, and act. But he was hundreds of miles away. Not that it would have made any difference if he had been home in Sherebury; I still couldn't have talked to him with no phone. But a part of me felt obscurely hurt, resentful that he was out of the country — in *Belgium,* of all ridiculous places! — when I needed him so badly.

"The fact remains, cat, that I'm in this all by myself, and will be until the phones are repaired. So there's really nothing I can do, is there?"

Stan considered the matter before strolling to the door and looking up at me.

"You want to go home, do you?" I got up to open the door, and then had a sudden thought. Yesterday, before I had climbed aboard my morbid train of thought, I had decided to go back to the hotel and help with their cleanup. What was to prevent my doing just that? I'd have to be careful what I said to Jake, but I could manage to avoid him, I thought, with all the work there was to be done.

What's more, if I kept my eyes and ears open, or could think of some clever questions to ask, I might just learn something.

It sure beat sitting around brooding.

"Wait till I get my jacket on, cat. I'm coming with you."

I didn't, of course, exactly "go with" Stan. A human is obliged to keep to the paths. But we ended up, more or less at the same time, at the hotel, which was alive with activity.

I waited in the road until I had spotted Jake, leaning rather precariously on a ladder and dealing with a shutter that was hanging by one hinge. I faltered, then. There he was, helping out, acting like the decent person he was. How could I . . .

That is not a productive thought, old girl. Stick to the program. I went around to the back of the house, where Chris and Janet were on their hands and knees in the garden.

Chris hailed me. "Dorothy! Join us, won't you? I can offer you potatoes, turnips, a few late carrots, or some particularly repellent parsnips."

I walked over. "Goodness! What a muddy mess!"

"Isn't it? That's why we're not trying to salvage any of the plants; they're goners. We're just gathering the roots for Hester and Andrew. We're all one big happy family now, fellow survivors, you see."

"You're in good spirits, I must say." I creaked to my knees, hitched up my jacket, and started sorting through lumps of mud for anything edible. Chris had helped me down with a considerate hand on my elbow; Janet had merely grunted, but at least she'd moved to make room for me.

Chris sobered. "Whistling in the dark, actually. We heard from Teresa's doctor this morning. They operated to try to relieve the pressure on the brain, but she's still not responding very well. We're trying to keep from thinking about it too much."

Well, I could understand that attitude only too well. There were a few thoughts I would rather avoid, myself. I shook my head and bent to the turnips.

I was glad when Janet finished up with what she considered to be her allocation of mud and went to another corner of the plot. It left Chris and me alone, nobody else within earshot, and as I dug I had worked out just what I wanted to ask him.

"Chris, you're going to think this is an odd question, but — do you know if something happened Monday night? With Bob?" Of course I had to leave Jake's name out of it, but I could reasonably ask about a murder victim, couldn't I?

Chris turned so pale I thought he was going to be sick. "What do you mean?" he asked with an unconvincing attempt at a smile.

So something *had* happened. "I don't know. I just — got the idea Bob was somehow involved in something peculiar. Can you tell me about it?"

"How did you know?"

It was almost a whisper, and I looked at him sharply.

"Chris, don't ask me, please. I can't tell you. And there's no reason why you should tell me anything at all, except that — well, it would be a very great help to me."

"It's your policeman friend, I suppose."

I sat back on my heels. "Now you've lost me. I haven't the faintest idea what you're talking about."

His color began to come back. "Oh. I thought — well, I suppose there's no reason why you shouldn't know. There wasn't anything to it, really, except that it made me mad, and I wasn't eager for it to get around."

"I won't tell anyone who — who doesn't have to know."

It was an ominous way to phrase it, and Chris went pale again, but he sighed.

"I guess it had to come out sooner or later. Bob made a pass at me, that's all. And I told him what I thought of him, him and his little boys, threw him out of my room, and slammed the door in his face. We probably woke Jake; his room's right across the hall. And that's all there was to it, and you can think what you like!"

I think I would have fallen if I hadn't been on my knees. "Little boys?" I managed to say, in what I hoped was an ordinary voice.

Chris was too upset to notice. "Yeah, those kids he had around all the time. If his interest was all fatherly, I'll eat this parsnip, mud and all."

"He was gay, then?"

Chris caught my tone, that time. He looked at me oddly.

"Not exactly. Or not exclusively, I should say. And he wouldn't admit it. At least that was the word in the gay community. He'd never come on to me before; I couldn't stand the guy. And that's why . . ."

I got it, finally, and looked at him with pity. "Oh, Chris. You think I think — I mean, were you afraid I was going to accuse you of having something to do with Bob's death?"

He looked relieved, and very, very young. "You mean you don't think so? I — I've been worrying ever since it happened. He'd been acting funny all day, moody, and I was scared —"

"You thought he killed himself because you turned him down." It was time to get rid of innuendo and talk plainly. "You can take my word for it, he didn't. Of that I am absolutely sure. However, I'm glad you decided to tell me about your little — encounter. Now I — I think I really must get up while I still can."

He hauled me to my feet, surprised me by planting a rather gritty kiss on my cheek, and went back to his work while I escaped into the house with a large basket of vegetables, to wash my hands and try to settle my mind.

I found Grace in the kitchen, surrounded by a huge pile of carrots and potatoes.

"Oh, good, more. Put them down there; I'll deal with them."

"Heavens, you're *glad* to have them? I'd think you'd never want to see another muddy vegetable again."

"They're food. If you had seen as much hunger as I have, you might feel differently about anything edible." She returned to her work, and I began to work at her side. Act normal.

I had all the pieces now. I knew about the

conversation Jake had overheard, that had put the match to the fuse. I still didn't know what to do about it, and I was no closer to an answer when Hester shooed us out of the kitchen so she could prepare lunch.

Grace and I, tired of standing, went to the lounge and sat. It was a sad room, with little furniture and no rugs. It would be days, perhaps weeks, before everything was dry and clean again. I more or less fell into a chair; Grace sat down more smoothly, but a little sigh of relief did escape her lips as she relaxed.

"I do believe you're as tired as I am, Grace. It certainly looks better on you than on me."

I was aware that my face was dirty, and that there was mud under my fingernails and on the knees of my slacks. My hair was uncombed. I was a mess.

Grace smoothed her skirt. Her hands, though wrinkled from being in water, were clean and well kept, and every silver hair on her head was smoothly in place. "I haven't been gardening. You look fine. It's honest dirt."

"Ah, but even when I'm clean, I can never achieve that effortless elegance you manage all the time. Your kind of beauty is in the bone; you'll be beautiful till the day you die."

She looked at me coolly, and then smiled a little. Perhaps it was because she was tired that she allowed her shell to crack a trifle. "I seldom receive such a delightful compliment. Thank you, Dorothy. It's all the more valuable because it seems totally disinterested, unlike those of — most people."

"Of whom?"

She gave me a long look, her smile wiped from her face.

"Please. I have a reason for asking. You had someone specific in mind, didn't you?"

She frowned a little, and then shrugged.

"Oh, I suppose it doesn't matter now. You're right, of course, though it applies generally, too. I am involved in a great deal of charity work, and I must also serve, often, as hostess for my husband's fund-raisers."

She saw my puzzled look. "Oh, that's right, you don't live in America anymore. My husband is an Illinois state senator. At any rate, my point is that I operate in many capacities in which a compliment is usually a veiled request, or a bribe, to put it less charitably. I have come to view my beauty as a burden rather than a gift."

I nodded. "I've often thought that really beautiful women must have rather a hard time of it, contrary to what most people would think. You'd never know when you were being appreciated for yourself."

"Yes. But I haven't really answered your question, have I? And you're waiting for me to tell all." She grimaced. "I dislike thinking about it, although it was a trivial business, really. It's simply that Mr. Williams — I cannot bring myself to call him 'Bob' — paid me a number of fulsome compliments Monday night, just before he attempted to — that is, he —"

She searched for a suitably delicate euphemism, while I vaguely remembered an odd little scene in the lounge that first night.

"He 'put the moves on you,' is, I believe, the way the young would put it."

"Exactly. The phrase has a certain vulgarity that precisely matches the fact. Not to mention the ludicrous side of it; I must be at least twenty years older than he was. I was, of course, disgusted, and told him to go take a cold shower."

That, I thought, made two pointed, personal rejections in one night. Bob was acceptable, apparently, to neither sex. I could understand why he had been moody the next day. Was it possible that I'd been wrong all along? Had he, in fact, committed suicide?

But again the tape replayed behind my

eyes. And again I saw him falling, quite definitely not jumping.

"Not to interrupt, but they said I should tell you lunch was ready. And I could maybe escort two lovely ladies to the dining room?"

Jake stood, beaming, in the doorway.

19

If I never have to suffer through a meal like that again, I won't be sorry. Hester, in gratitude for our help (and with her cooking pots returned to her), had produced an excellent lunch for us. The crab claws had probably come out of Iona Sound, and must have been sweet and tender. The bread was homemade and hot, the vegetables were perfectly cooked, and the dessert was some light, creamy concoction that looked like food for the gods.

Unfortunately, I couldn't eat. When Jake insisted I sit next to him, my stomach knotted into a hard little ball of misery, and my throat closed up every time I tried to take a bite. The longer he talked, with that twinkle in his eye, the more he flirted, impartially, with Grace and me, the closer the tears in my eyes came to spilling out. I lifted my wineglass, took the tiny sip that was all I could manage, and put it down again with an unsteady hand.

The other people in the room were in that excitable mood that follows a narrow escape from disaster, and my gloom was noticeable. It was Hattie Mae, of course, who drew everyone's attention to me. "You ain't eatin' nothin', Dottie!" she boomed out across the table.

I didn't even protest her corruption of my name. I'd had all I could stand; I pushed my chair back. "I'm sorry, Hester. This was lovely, but I'm afraid I'm not feeling very well. If you'll excuse me?"

Jake tried to go with me, but I brushed him off. "No, thanks, I have a really wicked headache, and I need to be alone. I'll be fine, and I'll see you all later."

It was true enough about my head. It was pounding so badly I was afraid I was going to be sick. But the worst malaise was in my soul.

The industrious villagers had already done a rough job of clearing the footpath. It wasn't perfect, but it was passable, and I was in a hurry. I pushed my way through, almost running, heedless of the twigs that caught at my sweater and the roots that tried to trip me. I was panting and almost sobbing when I reached my cottage, and my head was hurting worse than ever.

After I was sick — several times — I felt better. Or at least my head felt better. I drearily cleaned up my mess, changed into clean clothes, and then lay on my bed, hoping blessed sleep would come, and with it, oblivion.

I wasn't surprised to hear the knock at the door. I lay rigidly still, willing him to go away. He couldn't know for sure that I was awake.

"Mrs. Martin! Mrs. Martin, are you quite all right?"

The voice was gentle, male, English, and slightly familiar, although I couldn't place it. I dragged myself to the front window, opened it, and shouted, "I'll be right down." The tiny roof over the front door hid any view of my caller, but it certainly wasn't Jake. I went down and opened the door.

"I'm sorry to disturb you, but I saw you coming home, and you seemed to be in distress. I couldn't quite make up my mind whether I should interfere, but in the end . . ."

"Oh, do come in, Father — I mean Mr. — I'm sorry, I can't remember your name."

"Pym. Are you certain it isn't an intrusion?"

Suddenly I was quite sure. "Not at all. In fact, I think you may be exactly the person I need to talk to right now. Please sit down. Would you like some tea?"

"No, no, I've only just eaten my lunch. But if you —"

"What I need is some aspirin, actually. I'll be right back."

"I rather thought you looked as though you had a headache," said Mr. Pym when I had returned.

"It was a bad one, but it's passing, thank you. Now my problem is — well, I don't know what to do."

"Then tell me, and let me see if I can be of any help," he said simply, and sat back. His glasses were thick, but his nearsighted eyes were warm with understanding. I sat back, too, trying to put it all into words.

"Well — I suppose you heard about the tragedy? The young American who fell to his death in Fingal's Cave?"

He smiled gently. "Iona is a very small island, Mrs. Martin. Yes, I know about him. I have prayed for him every day since."

"He was murdered."

I hadn't meant to blurt it out quite that way, but Mr. Pym had been a priest for a long time; he wasn't easily startled.

"Indeed," he said mildly.

"I suppose you don't believe me." I sat up a little straighter and tried to stop sounding forlorn. "There's no reason why you should, really, but I'm afraid I do have some experience with murder."

I briefly recounted my unfortunate adventures in Shmerebury. "So you see, I think rather carefully before I make statements of that kind. Mr. Pym, I'm sure. And I know who did it." I couldn't keep the tears from my voice.

"I see. And you are — fond of this person?"

"I — yes, I am. He — oh, dear, I didn't mean to let you know even that much —"

"I am capable of keeping a great deal to myself. Indeed, I am often required to do so. You may tell me his name if you like, and be assured that I will tell no one else. But your very hesitation tells me that you are not certain you want to reveal his name to anyone."

He quirked his head to one side and studied me with those old eyes that couldn't see across the room, but saw so far into a human soul.

"That's just it, of course. No, I won't tell you his name, but I want to tell you about the circumstances. You see, I'm not sure he wasn't justified in what he did."

I explained all about Jake and his grandson. "Mr. Pym, he was all the poor man had, and he meant everything to him. And Bob must have been a real monster, preying on the children he was pretending to help. If he molested Aaron, he might have done it to others, and they might be infected, too. I think he — the murderer — felt it was more of an execution, a way of getting rid of a menace to society."

"Do you think so? Or are you letting your sympathy with the murderer cloud your judgment? Are you sure it was not quite simply an act of retribution?"

I studied my hands in my lap. "No," I said at last. "Of course I'm not sure. But what difference does it make? The police don't care much about motives."

"God cares, however. In fact, all that really concerns him about our actions is why we commit them. If we truly believe ourselves to be doing good, however mistakenly, God counts the action as good, even if it involves a crime for which human justice must punish us.

"And rightly so. That is, since human judges and juries can never truly know our souls, they must often pass judgment on actions alone. But the point of the question was not to make you feel guilty, as I see I have done."

My hands were twisting in my lap, and my eyes looked anywhere except into his.

"I was attempting, ineffectually perhaps, to help you make a decision about what you must do. You are not a judge, Mrs. Martin, nor a juror. You are bound in this particular instance by God's law, not by the laws concerning evidence and procedure and so on. Your dilemma, as I understand it, centers around what you must do with your knowledge."

"Especially since it's only guesswork. I could be very wrong —"

"But you believe you are right. So you must decide whether you are to turn this man, whom you perceive to be a decent, upright person, over to the authorities, or to say nothing and let him go on his way. Is that a fair statement of the problem?"

It was putting it more clearly and more brutally than I had permitted myself to do, but I nodded.

"Legally, of course, you know what the answer is. Morally, you may feel that the man was justified in what he did, and poses no danger to society, so that you may safely keep your ideas to yourself."

"No one else has any idea, you see!" I said eagerly. "It will be accepted as an accident, or just possibly as suicide, and forgotten."

"That has nothing whatever to do with your decision," said Mr. Pym sternly, "as you should know perfectly well. We are dealing here with what you ought to do, not with what you can get away with. It may not even be true that no one else suspects. But, true or not, it doesn't enter into the picture."

And then he simply waited in silence for me to think it through. It was a long silence, and my cheeks were wet when I finally broke it.

"You've answered it for me, haven't you? When you talked about my trying to 'get away with' something. I hadn't realized I was looking at silence as a sneaky option, but I was. I knew all along what I should do, didn't I?"

"The Platonic method has many merits," said Mr. Pym, with the hint of a smile. "One can take all the credit for a brilliant answer that always lay, in fact, in the mind of the questioner." He took my hands. "Don't be too distressed, my dear. The end result can safely be left in the hands of God, you know. Tell the truth and shame the devil, as the old saying has it. And to be quite practical about it, the actions of Scottish policemen and Scottish courts, when dealing with one American killing another, are apt not to be frightfully direct."

"I hadn't thought about that aspect of it, I admit. It does make me feel a little better. But, oh, Mr. Pym, he's such a *nice* man!" I was starting to cry in earnest, and Mr. Pym handed me a large handkerchief, rather shabby but quite clean.

"You'll feel better when you've cried it out of your system," he advised. "And then have yourself a good sleep; you've exhausted yourself, and we're never at our best when we're tired. I'm having a special service of Compline tonight at nine o'clock, in thanksgiving for our deliverance from the storm. Come if you like. They're lovely old prayers."

He let himself out the door, waving as I tried to thank him, and I followed his advice, went upstairs, and cried myself to sleep.

It was dark when I woke. I had apparently slept for hours. It was Friday evening, when the *ceilidh* had been planned, I suddenly remembered. There would be no *ceilidh* tonight; the island had little reason for merrymaking.

I sat up, stiffly. It was very cold in the bedroom, once I was out from under the duvet I had thrown over me, clothes and all.

Mechanically, I went about the small chores that had to be done. Lighting a fire was the first job; I had to take the chill off the house. I heated the soup and ate it, made coffee and drank it. Soon I would have to buy more oil and charcoal; I made a note on the pad I had put back by the telephone and even remembered I would have to ask for "paraffin," the Brit word for kerosene.

I had put my earlier notes in the fire. There was no point in keeping them. Every salient point was burned into my brain. Soon — tomorrow, perhaps, if the telephone people could get a new cable laid — I could notify the authorities of my conclusions and wash my hands of the whole affair.

I wished I hadn't thought of that particular phrase. I was feeling like Judas anyway. Echoes of Pontius Pilate didn't help.

I wasn't going to cry anymore. Weeping had been replaced by a sorrow beyond tears. I could not weep, for all the horrors of our society, for all the crimes beyond punishment and the sins seeking no redemption. I could not, anymore, even weep for Jake. He had done what he thought he must do. Now I would do what I thought I must. And may God be merciful, I thought bleakly.

I added my warmest sweater to the layers I already had on, and decided, a little before nine, to go to Compline, more because I was restless than out of any hope that it would bring me relief. There was no relief for me until my duty was done, and perhaps not then. Perhaps not ever. This was a terrible thing I had committed myself to do. For the first time I appreciated the enormous debt society owes to the police and the justice system, who take these life-and-death decisions out of the hands of ordinary people like me.

I had, twice before in my life, been instrumental in hunting down a murderer. In both cases they'd been people I knew, at least slightly. But they hadn't been especially admirable, and their crimes had been brutal, their motives petty. I had felt very little remorse when I'd brought about their downfall.

But this — this was different. Logically, it shouldn't matter that I approved of the villain far more than the victim. Murder was murder, and it was the ultimate crime, and it had to be punished. It was simple cowardice to wish that I were not the instrument.

I put my coat on, checked the fire to make sure it was safe, blew out the lamp, and stepped outside my door.

I would have gone back in immediately for the flashlight I'd forgotten, if the touch on my arm hadn't frozen me in my tracks.

"Ah! And you'd like to go for a walk with me, maybe, it's such a fine night?"

20

I didn't think, my brain had stopped. I turned and ran. The clouds were clearing, and there was a glimpse of the moon now and then, enough, when it was visible, to show me where I was going. Perhaps I had walked that village street enough in the past few days that I had some muscle memory, or perhaps the angel that is said to watch over fools kept me from tripping. The occasional lamp in a cottage window helped, too, and once I neared the jetty, the tittle cafe's lights were showing; they must, I thought as I tore past, have their own generator.

I couldn't keep up the pace for long. My wind was better than it would have been a week ago, from the sheer amount of walking and climbing I'd been doing, but it still wasn't terrific, and nothing short of a transplant was going to help my knees. I slowed once I had passed the cafe, but I kept going, glancing behind me every few steps.

The glances were pointless, of course. An army could have been following me and I wouldn't have seen them, unless they happened to stand in the middle of the street during a moonlit interval. Anyone with the sense to keep to the shadows would be invisible.

How did he know? What told him I knew his secret? Maybe I'd given myself away at lunch, acting so upset. Maybe something I'd said, some question I'd asked, had been repeated to him, and he'd understood.

Maybe — oh, dear heaven — maybe I'd told him just now, by running away! I'd done it to myself! If I'd had the sense to respond to his greeting coolly, agree that it was a lovely night but, unfortunately, I was going to church —

It was indeed, I realized as I stopped in a dark doorway for breath, a nice night. Brisk, as befitted late September, but no wind or rain, and the moon was making more and more headway against the clouds. Tomorrow would probably be a beautiful day, if by any chance I should live to see it.

I was cursing the moon, now, every time it showed its full face. The last wispy clouds would soon vanish, leaving the sky to the mercy of that spotlight. I was reminded of a book I'd once read, quoting a legend about goddesses or someone reeling in the moon for two weeks out of every month, gradually making the night dark, safe for anything that was fleeing a hunter. How I wished the moon-spinners were working tonight!

For tonight I was the quarry, and the hunter could find me quite easily.

I heard a step, the crunch of gravel somewhere behind me. I left the road, kept to the grass, and ran as fast as I could.

I'd been a fool, of course. The thought came to me as I ran, raggedly and with panting breath that could probably be heard all the way down to the jetty. If I had only headed the other way, to the church or the Abbey, or taken the footpath up to the hotel, or gone in almost any other direction than the one I had chosen, I would have reached people, and therefore safety, very quickly. It was the instinct to put as much distance as possible between me and Jake that had sent me this way. And this way lay only hills and moors and sheep pastures and, eventually, the sea.

With a great many places where I could fall, or get bogged down in a mire, or twist an ankle.

That thought, and the noise behind me, brought me to a stop. He was following, but slowly now, depending more on hearing than sight. I realized that my dark clothing kept me from being quite as visible as I had feared, and if I could only go quietly, perhaps on hands and knees . . . I dropped down, wriggled as silently as I could into a little depression, and tried to think.

I didn't know where I was, for sure. I thought perhaps I was on the Machair, the broad, grassy moor. If so, I was in a bad position. Aside from the occasional sand trap set up for the golf course, the Machair presented no hiding places. If I could just get up into the hills, which ought to lie close by, to my left (unless I'd lost my sense of direction completely), there would be a little cover. I could scooch down and pretend to be a rock, or something.

Jake didn't know the terrain any better than I did; that was one comfort. He could get just as thoroughly lost as I. If I was given any luck at all, I might be able to circle around and get back to the village or the hotel while he was still wandering the moors or getting lost in the hills. I had a chance, not maybe a very good one, but any chance is better than none.

He was getting closer, and my hollow was a poor excuse for a hiding place. It was time to move.

As exercise for the senior citizen, I do not recommend crawling through a Scottish sheep pasture, especially at night. I tried to move when the moon was behind a cloud and freeze when it came out, so I kept finding nice, sharp rocks with my knees, and then having to kneel on them indefinitely until some obliging cloud set me free for a few moments. The Machair, when I had crossed it earlier in the week, had seemed like a lovely, soft, grassy field. In the dark, on all fours, it more closely resembled a gravel pit. I tried hard not to think of the other hazards, left by the sheep, that my bare hands were doubtless encountering.

I was making for a wire fence that ought to appear on my left any time now. The path up to the loch lay next to that fence, if I remembered correctly, and there were, in its vicinity, any number of little hillocks and large rocks that might provide a hiding place.

There were also any number of small rocks, and no grass to cushion them. I wouldn't think about them, either, not just now. Sufficient unto the day is the evil thereof.

Oh, Hattie Mae would be proud of me!

Someday I may be able to forget the terrors of the next few hours. I found the fence without difficulty, and followed it up the hill, in a kind of crouch that caused excruciating pain to nearly every part of my anatomy, but I couldn't crawl anymore, not with the path simply *all* rocks. Every now and then a tenacious bog provided a little variety in the dreadfulness; my shoes were soaked with water, and threatened occasionally to be pulled off by some particularly gluey patch. I worried about the noise I was making. A gravely path scrunches, and bogs squelch, and there's no help for it. If Jake heard me, I'd just have to — do something else. I prayed I could figure out what.

I was also praying that any dogs at the farm I was passing slept well at night. I hadn't seen dogs when we passed on our pilgrimage, but there were bound to be some. You can't run sheep without a dog. And if they barked and woke the farmer, I could be dealing with a double-edged sword. He might believe me, and take me in — but, equally, he might think I was a lunatic and send me packing. In either case, Jake would be quite sure where I was.

I toiled up the hill.

At one point, shortly before I reached the loch at the crest of the hill, I had an inspiration. There was, I remembered vaguely, some sort of small building up here. If I had thought about it at all before, as preoccupied as I had been with Jake's troubles, I had thought it probably had something to do with the pumping of water for Iona's supply. Now I thought of it as sanctuary. If I could reach it, and if by some miracle of Iona's trusting nature, the door was unlocked . . .

I never got the chance to find out. The building was in a fenced enclosure, and the gate was securely padlocked. The moon was shining strongly by that time, and I could just see that the top wire of the fence was barbed. Evidently, trust did not extend to something as precious as water. I bitterly cursed the (presumed) vandals who had made these precautions necessary, and sat down by the fence to consider my next move.

I couldn't go on much farther. I didn't know how long I'd been creeping along, but it was too long for my bones and muscles. Every arthritic joint — which included most of the joints I possessed — was screaming at me, and some were near the point of locking up in protest. This was madness. There must be some rock, some niche, *something* to shelter me until — well, until I could figure out what to do about this ridiculous predicament.

For it was beginning to seem ridiculous, two people of our ages, Jake's and mine, crawling around on a Scottish hillside in what seemed like the middle of the night. He wasn't James Bond, for goodness' sake, and I wasn't some lithe Russian spy. Exactly what was I afraid of? He didn't own a gun, or a knife. Oh, all right, I didn't know that for certain, but *Jake?* Trying to kill *me?* No, it was too silly.

I sat and listened. There was no sound in the night, save for an occasional odd crunching that I knew was some sheep having himself a late snack of coarse grass, and the distant crash of the surf against some of the rocks below me.

With a good deal of maneuvering, and a number of little moans and grunts, I stood up.

"Dorothy! So there you are! No, wait — so can I talk to you, already?"

We can't control reflexes. I was running wildly down the hill before he had finished the first syllable.

I will probably bear some of the scars of that reckless plunge till the day I die. I was lucky, I suppose, that I broke no bones. It's always foolish to run downhill, and in rocky, unfamiliar terrain, and in the dark, it's suicidal. I fell, many times, but I managed to scramble up again each time and keep going. I had no idea where I was, and I didn't care. I had to get away from that voice that kept calling me.

"Dorothy! Hey, slow down! *Dorothy!*"

I was gaining ground. He sounded farther

away now, and his voice sounded strained and breathless.

He shouldn't be doing this, with his heart condition, I thought, and then shook myself, mentally. He killed a man, remember? He maybe tried to kill Teresa, and for sure he's trying to kill you, Dorothy Martin, so stop feeling sorry for him.

But the thought had taken my concentration away from what I was doing for just that crucial moment. I took a step into nothing, tried to shift my balance, fell, and went rolling down a steep slope, striking rocks as I went, grabbing at weeds that tore away in my hands.

When I came to a stop, pained and dizzy, it took a few moments to realize I was still alive. Checking everything I could, I decided I was more or less intact, though bleeding gently from a hundred cuts and scrapes. For a wonder, I was sprawled on something relatively soft and smooth.

The moon was directly overhead, and when I was able to sit up and look around, I realized where I was.

I was lying in a small grassy hollow in the one place on Iona I had decided I would never visit again.

The marble quarry.

"Dorothy, where are you? Are you all

right? Answer me, can't you?"

It was over. The infirmities of age had caught up with me. I couldn't run anymore. I probably couldn't even stand up. I sighed and shifted to a slightly more comfortable position. Might as well not die sitting on a sharp rock.

"I'm over here, Jake."

21

My voice was steady as I called out a few more times to help Jake find me. Now that the game was lost, why not cooperate?

He slithered down the bank and collapsed by my side, panting. I waited with a certain amount of interest to see what form my demise was going to take. Fear was gone; I was simply too tired. In fact, it occurred to me, as I sat and listened to Jake's breathing slow down to normal, that I had never before in my life actually comprehended what the word "exhausted" meant.

Even after he seemed to have recovered, he was slow to speak, and when he did, his voice was sad and his words were the last ones I expected to hear.

"Why did you run away from me?"

I turned and stared at him. His face, white in the moonlight, looked unutterably weary and bleak.

"Why are you afraid of me?" he asked again.

This time I could answer. "You killed Bob Williams."

"I did what?" He sounded as though he had simply misunderstood me.

"Oh, I understand why. I even — well, you probably thought you were justified, and maybe —"

"*What* did you say I did?"

"Oh, Jake, I don't want to say it again!"

"Say it again. So maybe I didn't hear you right."

"You murdered Bob Williams."

"And how did I do that, when he was alone? You saw what happened. He fell."

"Yes, but — the water. You spilled the water on the rocks, and left him to fall."

There was a very long pause. My heart-beat drummed in my ears.

"So you maybe thought I was going to kill you?" Jake said finally, with that ironic intonation I had gotten to know so well. "Why?"

"Because you knew I knew! Teresa had caught on, somehow, and you tried to keep her quiet . . ."

This time the silence went on even longer.

"All right," he said, in a voice with all the life gone out of it. "You think you know so much about what happened that day, maybe I'd better tell you all of it.

"It started the night before, the Monday night. There was a lot of activity going on in that quiet, respectable little hotel Monday night, did you know?"

"I heard about some of it."

"Yeah, well, did anybody tell you that my room was straight across the hall from Chris's?"

"Yes. When I learned that, I knew what did it for you."

"Yeah, well. I was in bed, and I tried not to listen, believe me. At my age I need my sleep. But he would've waked the dead, he and Chris, going at it hammer and tongs, in whispers, but the kind that can carry to the third balcony.

"The names Chris called him I won't repeat to a lady, but they were enough to give me the idea. Chris said —"

He stopped abruptly, apparently to rephrase his thoughts.

"Chris implied that Bob was — maybe a little too fond of some of the children he worked with, and I tell you, that woke me up. I spent the rest of the night trying to piece the thing together, and I came up with a whole picture every time. So the next day I went after him. I had some questions to ask."

"In the cave."

"In the cave. I didn't plan it that way, it was just the first time I could get the bastard by himself. He might be innocent, see? I couldn't see how, but he might be. And it wouldn't be fair to accuse him in front of other people."

"And he said . . . ?"

"Oh, at first he denied the whole thing, of course, said I had a filthy mind and I was a disgrace to my calling, and like that. And then I told him a thing or two about what I'd heard the night before, and who was calling who a disgrace, and he turned, like a cornered rat. He said, okay, what did I think I could do about it? And he was going to die, anyway, from his disease, and was I going to blacken the name of a dying man? And more of the same. Ah, I tell you, it made me sick to my stomach, the way he'd bluster and then whine, whine and then bluster. So —" there was a pause, and I could just see one of his elaborate shrugs "— so I left."

"After you'd dumped water on the rocks."

"No. I don't know what you're talking about, wet rocks. The rocks were dry."

So was my mouth. "But . . . but, Jake, they were wet when I saw Bob fall. That's why he fell! Maybe you didn't do it on purpose —"

"I didn't have any water with me in the cave. I'd drunk it all. I wished I had some, to take the taste of Bob Williams out of my mouth. And I don't know what you're talking about, with Teresa."

It was a flat denial, and it had the ring of absolute truth. "But . . . but then . . . oh, dear God!"

I sat in an appalled silence. What had I done?

I had met a man, a good man who had been dealt unbearable blows by life. We had become friends, he had confided in me. And I, with my interfering nature, my love of prying into other people's business, had drawn a superficial conclusion and accused him of murder.

"Jake, I . . . I'm so sorry . . ."

I stopped because there were no adequate words. I'm sorry I was afraid of you. I'm sorry I thought you were a murderer. I'm sorry your life was destroyed by someone who really was a monster. I'm sorry you've gone through hell.

"Yeah." Jake sat, hunched into himself. And the night grew colder.

After an eternity, Jake stood up. "We should maybe go back, huh? We'll freeze out here."

"I don't think I can," I said drearily, trying to keep my teeth from chattering. "It's so far, and my knees . . . and the moon is about to set. We could get lost . . . but you go. You've got a compass, and you can move faster without me. I'll be all right until morning."

"No, you won't," he said flatly. "Okay, I'll see what I can do."

He tossed me his jacket and walked away before I could protest. I wrapped the coat around my legs, which were wet from all the times I had fallen into bogs, and prepared to wait out however much of the night I had to, until Jake could bring help.

He was back in five minutes. "I've found something. Can you get up?"

"I guess so, but what —"

"Over there." He helped me to my feet, his arm as steady as the top of a fence, and as impersonal.

He had found, a few feet away, what amounted to a little cave. Or hardly that, just a recess in the rock wall, one of the sides of the grassy depression we were in. What made it especially good was that there was a slab of rock, marble quarried years ago, presumably, leaning at a slant in front of it, like a door.

"We'll be warm in there, with that slab cutting off the wind. Have you got any matches?"

"I don't think so." I patted myself down and finally came up with a box in my pants pocket. I must have dropped them in when I lit the lamp. "Yes, I do. There won't be any dry wood, though, after the storm."

"Not wood, peat. This whole island is peat, and that stuff'll smolder, even wet. I'll be right back."

And so it was that, an hour or so later, we had a small fire going. It emitted a great deal more smoke than heat, but it showed no signs of going out, and it did help take the chill off the night. I settled down with my back to the stone wall, and when Jake thought the fire no longer required his attention, he joined me.

"Jake, I — there's nothing I can say to make up for —"

"Sleep," he said wearily. "It won't be long till morning. We'll be warmer if we stay together." He put that dispassionate arm around me, and I tried to follow his advice.

I didn't sleep well. My mind was in turmoil, I was cold and in pain, and I kept waking up to wriggle into a new position that might simulate comfort. Every time, Jake was there, cushioning my head, holding me close for warmth.

Toward dawn I fell into a sounder sleep. My last thought was to wonder how I could ever have supposed this man a murderer.

Someone was snoring, very loudly. I wished they would be quiet so I could sleep. And this was an awfully hard bed, and where were all the covers —

I woke, shivering, sore all over. The snoring noise was getting louder.

It was a helicopter, and it was landing — I craned my neck — surely it was landing just on the other side of the hill. Who? Why?

And where was Jake?

I called, but I couldn't be heard over the beat of the rotor, so I stood up.

The words do not begin to convey the struggle. I thought at first that I actually would not be able to make my bones and muscles obey me, that I would simply have to sit there until someone picked me up, joints locked into position, and carried me to some place where I could be worked loose, like the Tin Man. But eventually, one impossible movement at a time, I got to my feet, ducked out of the little cave, and looked around.

I remembered the place, now that I could see where I was. It was on the edge of the marble quarry proper, just before one got to the horrible rusting hulks of machinery. I had rested here, the day of the pilgrimage. My New Age acquaintance had sat pontificating almost in the very spot where Jake and I had found shelter, such as it was, for the night.

The helicopter had shut itself down, and

peace reigned once more. "Jake! Jake, where are you?"

There was only silence, and the soft sigh of the wind, and that crunching noise of sheep feeding. I stamped out what little remained of our pitiful fire, and sat down on the bank to wait for Jake to return. He would tell me what was happening; I was incapable of climbing the hill to find out for myself.

The sun was still low, but it promised warmth soon. The day was going to be beautiful, in fact, the kind of autumn day that seems to relent, to say it was all a mistake, summer isn't going to be taken away after all. When you're young, you trust the promises and forget about the winter to come until it is upon you. Even when you're old enough to recognize autumn as the liar he is, though, you can enjoy the beautiful lies as you enjoy the line fed you by a charmer. He doesn't mean a word of it, and you know it, but it's pleasant to pretend you believe.

It's especially pleasant to weave fantasies when facing reality is pretty painful.

"Jake!"

The crunching sounds were getting louder, and I finally realized they were feet on rocks, not sheep.

"Jake?" Had he gone for help, after all?

"Dorothy!"

And then my muscles, which could barely move at all a few minutes before, were letting me run and climb —

— and throw myself into Alan's open arms.

There were a few minutes of babbled incoherencies, a lot of hugging, and one extremely proficient kiss before Alan held me away from him at arm's length and demanded, "Are you all right?"

"Of course I am! Now," I added, robbing my original reply of all its force. "Except I'm cold."

"Help is on the way," Alan said with a broad grin. He hugged me close again and nodded to the path behind him.

Struggling up the rocky trail, their arms laden, were a uniformed man, probably the helicopter pilot, and — I rubbed my eyes and looked again — Lynn Anderson, dressed for London in a very smart pants suit, a silk shirt, and neat little designer boots that were at the moment scarred and filthy with mud.

"Lynn! What on earth . . . ?"

"We'll save explanations for later, shall we?" said Alan. "I brought hot coffee and blankets. Here."

He took the thermos the pilot handed

him, unscrewed the top, and poured me some. I took it gratefully, wrapped my hands around it, and sipped. It was a little sweeter than I like my coffee, but boiling hot, and — I looked at Alan doubtfully.

"Brandy? At this hour of the morning?"

He draped a blanket around my shoulders and grinned again. "You are leading a dissipated life, aren't you, my dear? Out all night, drinking before the sun is well up — tsk, tsk. Finish that, and then we'll see how we're going to get you to the bird."

"Get *us* to the bird," I amended. "Jake should come with us. His heart isn't really up to all this climbing."

"Ah, yes, who is Jake? You were calling for him when I first came up the path."

"You said we'd save explanations for later. He's — a friend, and he probably saved my life last night. But he was gone when I woke up. I think he started back to the village for help, but it's dangerous alone; there are bogs and cliffs and things, not to mention his heart. You must have seen him from the helicopter."

"We didn't see anyone until we spotted you — and we wouldn't have done that if it hadn't been for your fire."

"But — he couldn't have been gone very long! Oh, Alan, he must have fallen, or . . ." I trailed off. I didn't want to say aloud any of the other possibilities. I didn't even want to think them. "Can't you send the helicopter to look again?"

Alan looked at me a little oddly, and then at the pilot, who nodded.

"Piece of cake. But we ought to get the lady back home first, right?"

"No, Alan, please, I'm worried about Jake. I'll be fine. Please!"

22

After the pilot had left, there was an awkward little pause. Lynn poured me some more coffee, which I sipped absently. The sun was living up to its promise; I was almost warm.

Alan paced back and forth, avoiding my eyes. Lynn, on the other hand, was watching me closely, looking away only when I happened to glance up.

"Oh, all right!" I burst out finally. "I'm here because I was an idiot! I was on a wild goose chase, only I was the goose. And I'm tired and sore and I was never so glad to see anyone in my life as I was to see Alan — to see both of you — this morning, but that's absolutely all I'm going to say until we find Jake and this is over!"

"Will you at least tell us who Jake is?" asked Alan with heavy patience.

I knew what was the matter with him, of course, but I wasn't about to go into a full explanation until we were alone. If he was going to stew, he'd just have to stew.

I did what I could.

"Jake is a rabbi. Jacob Goldstein. And if I

told you his life story — well, he's had more trouble in his life than most twenty people.

"He's from Chicago. He's on Iona with a bunch of other Americans. One of them fell and drowned in Fingal's Cave on Tuesday. Well, I guess you know about that, somehow. And not to be inquisitive, but what *are* you doing here, anyway?"

That did it. Alan had relaxed, his face gentler. And Lynn collapsed into giggles. "What are we doing here, she asks!" said Lynn, rolling her eyes skyward, "She wants to know why we came!"

Alan sat down and put his arm around me, muttering, "You and your lame ducks," in my ear. To Lynn he said mildly, "Why don't you tell her?"

"My *dear!* After making about fifteen desperate phone calls, and leaving dire messages left and right, and then getting caught in a hurricane and not being reachable, you wonder why your friends were worried about you! When Tom and I got your messages, we tried to call you back, but your phone was out of order. So we called Jane, and she told us about the storm, and *she* called Alan, and he told her what he had learned —"

"What do you mean, what he had learned?" I asked, more relaxed myself, but thoroughly confused by now. I turned to him. "What *had* you learned?"

"Well, my dear, Jane and I had been talking. She was rather concerned about you, and intimated that you'd managed to entangle yourself with a body. Again."

I felt that the "again" was unnecessary, and said so.

"So I felt that I should do a little checking," said Alan smoothly, ignoring me. "Your telephone was still working at that point, but you were at neither the cottage nor the hotel. And the more I considered the situation, the less I liked it. Fortunately, I had other resources at my command. I rang Derek — you remember Derek Morrison, don't you, from the Town Hall mess — and he got in touch with Glasgow."

"Glasgow! Do you mean to tell me you were talking about me — I mean, Inspector Morrison was talking about me — to the police in *Glasgow?*"

He had the grace to look embarrassed. "Derek assured me that he mentioned your name only tangentially, as a witness to a death, so that they could find it in the computer. However, when he was told that the case remained open, and that no determination had yet been made about whether a crime was committed, he became uneasy, and I had to admit he had reason, given your —"

"Alan . . . " My voice rose, warningly.

"— your predilection for looking into anything that seems peculiar. But of course by the time Derek had gathered all this information, and passed it along to me, you were in the midst of a world-class gale, and incommunicado. So the best thing seemed to be to come and see for myself."

"Well, the police have decided now. There was no crime." My tone of voice had changed, and they looked at me with concern. Time to change the subject; this conversation was getting too near the bone. "But how did you get a police helicopter? I thought they'd all be out there rescuing people, and anyway, you don't have any jurisdiction here, do you?"

"Not officially, no, though all the police forces in the kingdom are supposed to cooperate with one another. But I thought it would take a great deal of time to convince Glasgow of the need for urgency. So I rang Lynn back and told her what I proposed to do, and Tom put one of his company's helicopters at my disposal. When I flew back to England, they met me at Gatwick, and here we are. Simple."

Simple, indeed. Combine English authority with American efficiency and the clout wielded by the wealthy executive of a multinational corporation, and you can get several people to a remote island in the Hebrides in no time at all.

"Well," I said with elaborate nonchalance, "of course I'm delighted to see you all — where's Tom, by the way?"

"Back at the cottage," said Lynn. "He wanted to come along, but the doctor has absolutely forbidden strenuous exercise for a while, and we already knew how far away you were — we flew over the whole island as soon as we found out you weren't at the cottage or the hotel, and nobody had seen you for a while. So I made him stay back there and rest. He was *wild!*"

"And he's probably having himself something totally inappropriate for breakfast. Well, as I said, I'm so glad you're finally here, but as you can see, I'm fine. I wasn't in need of rescue after all. It's Jake who —"

I stopped. I had heard the beat of the helicopter's rotors.

We waited, silently, while the sound grew louder and nearer and finally stopped. It seemed a long time before we heard the crunch of gravel on the path, and longer still until the pilot appeared, with Jake trailing behind him.

His shoulders were bowed, his steps labored. He looked like an old man.

But he was alive. I released my breath; I hadn't realized until then that I had been holding it.

"Alan," said Lynn, "don't you think you and I and Scott, here, had better go back to the chopper and radio for a boat? There's a little harbor just down there —" she pointed "— and it would be easier for Jake and Dorothy than having to climb over that hill again."

I shot her a glance of appreciation. It didn't take three of them to operate the radio. Lynn can be very intuitive.

So Jake and I were left alone, sitting side by side in the sun to wait for transportation.

"Where did you go?" I asked when I dared.

"Away. To think." He raised his head and looked at me over the tops of his glasses. "It was almost morning. I figured you'd be okay."

"Oh, Jake!" I didn't know whether to laugh or cry. "When I woke up and saw you were gone, I was so worried about you. I was afraid — where did the helicopter find you?"

He waved vaguely. "Over there. Not far. There are cliffs . . ."

I sucked in my breath sharply, and tried to

cover it with a cough. "Cliffs, Jake?"

"Yeah." He looked at me directly for the first time. "Yeah. Why not?"

"Because people would miss you, for one thing."

"Like who?"

"Your friends. Me, for one." ·

He grunted. "Sure. You're such a good friend you thought I was a murderer."

I put a hand on his arm. "Jake, listen. You have to understand. Nothing I can say will make up for my utter stupidity. I know that. But back before I lost my mind, I knew you were one of the most decent, really good people I'd ever met. Even after I — came to my dumb conclusion, I kept trying to justify what I thought you did. You don't deserve any of the awful things that've happened to you and you certainly didn't deserve my — my asinine accusations."

"So what in the hell could make you think —"

"I — it was the water that started me off. The rocks were wet when Bob fell, Jake. And I couldn't understand how they got that way. And then I — well, I thought you had a good reason to want him dead, and when Teresa got so much worse when you were taking care of her, and started babbling about water, I thought maybe she'd seen you, and you — Anyway, I put two and two together and made five."

Jake had been listening closely, and now he sighed and pulled at his beard. I sat, tears slipping down my checks.

Finally he sighed again, patted my hand, and nodded soberly. "So you added wrong. But you had your math right up till then. It makes sense."

I sat up and looked at him incredulously. "That's — very generous of you, Jake. I —"

"So what I want to know," he went on, "is, why *was* Teresa talking about water all the time?"

I stared at him, my eyes widening, my mind racing. "She always carried water," I said in a breathy voice.

"And she was right outside the cave when I left," said Jake. "She could have heard. I didn't talk to her; I wasn't in the mood for talking, so I went the other way and sat on the rocks for a while, down by the edge of the water."

"She was sort of odd when I met her a little later, too," I remembered. "Sort of — exhilarated. Surely if she'd just set a trap for someone she wouldn't . . ."

Jake shook his head. "She wouldn't set a trap for someone. Any more than I would."

Well, I deserved that. "No," I agreed, and

looked at my lap until I remembered something else. "Just after Bob fell," I said slowly, "I thought I saw someone at the mouth of the cave. It wasn't you?"

Jake shook his head again.

"Then this is what I think happened." I paused to sort it out.

"Listen, and tell me if I'm making things up out of whole cloth again. I think Teresa heard your fight with Bob, in the cave. She was already annoyed with him, and I'll bet she went charging in, furious. She's got a terrible temper, I know that for sure. Just suppose he acted the way he did with you, justifying himself and pretending to be pitiable. It would be just like her to throw something. Say, an open bottle of water?"

Jake nodded cautiously.

"And then she tore out of there. She was running when I met her; she almost knocked me down. It could have been that rush of adrenaline you get when you've had a really good fight. The rest of the world looks wonderful for a while. But just about then I heard some other people say something about the rocks being dangerous when they're wet. What if Teresa heard it, too? What would she have done?"

"Teresa's okay, y'know," said Jake soberly. "There's a good Catholic conscience behind all that belligerence. She'd worry about Bob — and about you. She'd turn back to warn you."

"So she'd see Bob fall, and know what caused it. And she'd convince herself it was pure accident, and he deserved it anyway — until she got a bump on the head and that good Catholic conscience you mentioned took over."

Jake nodded again. Just for a moment he looked like one of the old patriarchs, Abraham or Solomon or Moses, passing judgment.

"So what do we do about it?"

I could have hugged him for the "we." "I vote for doing nothing," I said. "I've already done more than enough on unsupported conjecture, don't you think? We can't ask her about it while she's unconscious, and if it happened the way we think, it really was an accident, after all. Her only guilt was in not saying anything afterward."

"Guilt enough," said Jake gruffly. "Made a couple of us pretty miserable for a while."

I held out a hand in apology; he took it in forgiveness. We sat, absorbed in our own thoughts, warm in the sun, until the hoot of a boat told us we could go back to civilization.

23

It wasn't until hours later that Alan and I had a chance to talk alone. First Tom had to be told the whole story of my "rescue," with dramatic embellishments from Lynn. Then the crowd from the hotel gathered. I related a bowdlerized tale I'd invented; I'd gone walking, stupidly, alone at night. Jake had seen me go and followed, worried; we'd ended up too far away to get home. It was close enough, though Jake was uncomfortable with the heroic role thrust upon him. Mr. Pym dropped in to see how I was, and Maggie from the Heritage Centre, and Deirdre, and all the neighbors from the cottages in the village. Lynn finally shooed everyone out, including Alan, and put me to bed.

So it was mid-afternoon before I went downstairs and found Alan playing chess with Tom.

"Feeling better, are you?" asked Alan.

"Somewhat, thank you. I'm rested, anyway, although I wonder if I'll ever get back to normal steep patterns. And I'm so stiff I'm not sure I can move."

"Then let's go for a walk. It's a fine, warm day, and I promise we won't go far. You have to keep the muscles working, you know, or you *will* be in trouble."

"Slave driver."

But I pulled on my hat. I was glad to get out of the cottage, and the afternoon was lovely, warm but not hot, and very drowsy and still.

We walked up toward the hotel, talking aimlessly about Alan's accommodations at the Iona Hotel and Lynn's efforts to cook with no electricity. When we got to the Nunnery, Alan led me to a bench in the garden and sat me down. Our only company was the black-and-white cat, and, of course, the bees.

"Nice hat," said Alan.

"Good thing you like it. It's the only one I brought."

"You — with only one hat? No wonder you got into trouble."

I smiled and leaned back against his arm.

"Can you talk about it now?" he asked after a companionable silence.

I sat up, took a deep breath, and told him the whole sorry story. "It all begins with Jake, really . . ."

I told him about Bob, and his fall. I told

him about all the people in the Chicago contingent, and their foibles and their strengths. I told him about Aaron's life and death, and unwound for him my unwilling conclusions. Finally, I told him about my terror-stricken flight from Jake, my horror when I realized I was wrong, and our version, Jake's and mine, of what had really happened.

"You won't have to do anything about it, will you, Alan? Jake and I thought it was better left alone."

"Me? This is Scotland. I couldn't if I wanted to. Which I don't."

"I don't know whether to hope Teresa gets well, or not. I don't think I ever want to know for sure —"

"Your friend Mr. Pym would tell you to leave it to God, and he's probably quite right."

There was a rather solemn, but comfortable, silence.

"I don't suppose they'll ever find Bob."

"Mmm. I had a little word with the police today, by radio. They've called off the search for the body — there's no point, apparently, after such a storm — and marked the investigation closed. The Chicago people can go home as soon as they can get a plane from Glasgow. Listen, Dorothy."

His tone of voice had changed, sharpened with intensity. I sat up straighter, surprised. "What?"

"Dorothy, will you marry me? Soon?"

I sat, dumb.

"You cannot imagine what I've been through, not knowing what kind of trouble you were getting into, not being able to see you, or talk to you, or help you. I don't ever, ever want to be put in that position again. I know you hadn't quite made up your mind, and I didn't intend to rush you, but — my God, woman, I can't live this way!"

The black-and-white cat jumped down and scurried away. I found my voice.

"Alan, this whole week I've been missing you and trying to reach you. All I wanted to do was talk to you, get your advice, hand the whole situation over to you. And when I heard your voice coming over the hill today, for a minute I thought I'd died and gone to heaven. Yes, of course I'll marry you — as soon as you like. Can we do it here — on Iona? In spite of — everything —" my voice caught for a moment and then steadied "— this is a special place for me."

He pulled me to him, his arm around my shoulder. "I wish we could, but there's the little matter of a license. It'll have to be back in Shrebury, I'm afraid. Or in Indiana, of course, if you'd rather —"

"No, you don't," I said firmly. "You said soon. Don't renege. Sherebury, as soon as we get back. And Alan — in case I never said so before — I do love you. A lot."

He laughed hugely and turned my face to his. I'm quite sure the Nunnery, in all its hundreds of years of chaste existence, never saw a kiss like that before.

The Campbells had a *ceilidh* for us that night, a before-the-wedding reception. Hester picked the few flowers that had survived the storm, and so did every other gardener; Janet arranged them, and the room looked lovely. Hattie Mae sang to Chris's accompaniment, including an extremely surprising version of "O Promise Me," and everyone kissed the bride-to-be; I got an enthusiastic buss from Jake. There was Highland dancing; I tried one easy reel with Alan and then just watched contentedly.

The Chicagoans left the next day. It was a Sunday, just a week (amazingly) after I had left Sherebury. We all went to the Abbey for an ecumenical service, and prayed in our own ways for Bob, and for Teresa, still unconscious in Oban. I said a fervent prayer for Jake, too; he was there, in a corner, his accustomed ironic smile on his face. Look out for him, please, God, even if he doesn't believe in You. He needs something worthwhile to do, something hard that will occupy all his time. Find it for him, will You?

Grace had, with her customary efficiency, arranged matters with the airline and the Chicago Religious Assembly; the group was going to catch a Monday morning flight at no extra charge, so they had to catch the Sunday 1:15 ferry from Iona. They'd stay in Oban for a couple of hours, to see Teresa, and then catch the last train to Glasgow. Alan and I walked down to the jetty to see them off.

Each of them shook our hands ceremoniously. Grace smiled graciously, Janet grunted something about being glad to get off this godforsaken island. Typical to the last.

Hattie Mae and Chris walked down to the boat together, arguing loudly about music. "I sure was glad to meet you, Dottie, honey," said Hattie Mae expansively before turning back to attack Chris's views. Chris merely winked as he shook my hand.

Jake was the last to board. He amazed me by kissing my hand with one of his little bows. "You're a lucky man," he said to Alan. "If you're ever in Chicago . . ."

"We'll look you up," I promised, and

meant it. "Good luck, Jake."

He shrugged and raised his~~eyebrows~~ and boarded the ferry.

The village was steeped in Sunday quiet as we walked back up the hill. Waves lapped at the jetty; seagulls mewed; shoals of sparrows swam in the still air. You could hear the beat of their wings.

We took the shortcut through the Nunnery grounds, and as we reached the garden, Alan paused.

"Dorothy, we'll be making some promises to each other soon. There's one I'd like now."

"And what might that be?"

"I'll be taking you for better or for worse. Will you please promise me that you'll limit the worse to no more murder and mayhem than can reasonably be expected?"

He was smiling; I looked up at him and grinned. "I promise I'll try."

Hand in hand, we walked up the peaceful road.

The employees of Thorndike Press hope you have enjoyed this Large Print book. All our Large Print titles are designed for easy reading, and all our books are made to last. Other Thorndike Press Large Print books are available at your library, through selected bookstores, or directly from the publishers.

For more information about titles, please call:

(800) 223-1244
   or
(800) 223-6121

To share your comments, please write:

Publisher
Thorndike Press
P.O. Box 159
Thorndike, Maine 04986